VEROI
in Arg
led he
city th
years.

Ⅴ

fondness for words, language and the magic of storytelling. She has an MA in Creative Writing from Kingston University.

Veronica currently lives in Buenos Aires with her husband, Ale, and her daughter, Tomiko. She teaches creative writing at Universidad de San Andres and is a contributing editor and writer for one of Argentina's leading news organizations.

When Veronica is not writing or teaching, she's either a) meditating or b) enjoying life with her family (which, in a way, is another beautiful way to meditate).

The Word-Keeper is her first novel.

THE
WORD-KEEPER

Veronica del Valle

SilverWood

Published in 2019 by SilverWood Books

SilverWood Books Ltd
14 Small Street, Bristol, BS1 1DE, United Kingdom
www.silverwoodbooks.co.uk

Copyright © Veronica Del Valle 2019
Illustrations © Eleanor Hardiman 2019

ISBN 978-1-78132-841-5 (paperback)
ISBN 978-1-78132-908-5 (ebook)

British Library Cataloguing in Publication Data
A CIP catalogue record for this book is available from the British Library

Page design and typesetting by SilverWood Books
Printed on responsibly sourced paper

For Tomiko

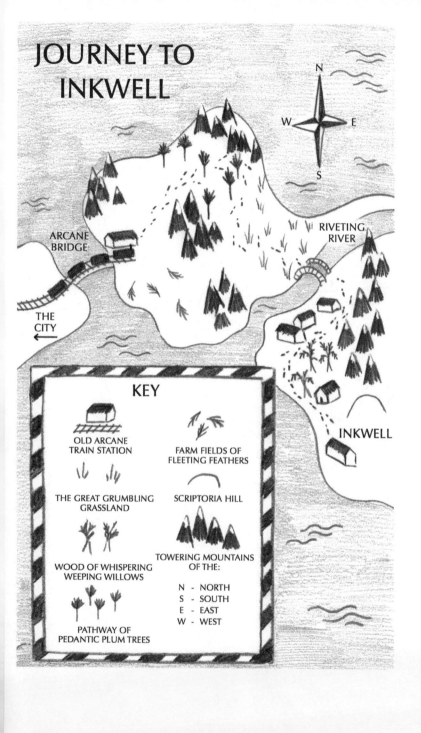

JOURNEY TO INKWELL

N
W   E
S

ARCANE
BRIDGE

RIVETING
RIVER

THE
CITY
←

INKWELL

KEY

OLD ARCANE
TRAIN STATION

FARM FIELDS OF
FLEETING FEATHERS

THE GREAT GRUMBLING
GRASSLAND

SCRIPTORIA HILL

WOOD OF WHISPERING
WEEPING WILLOWS

TOWERING MOUNTAINS
OF THE:

N - NORTH
S - SOUTH
E - EAST
W - WEST

PATHWAY OF
PEDANTIC PLUM TREES

This is a simple story. But the fact that it's simple does not make it less important. The power of words must never be underestimated, for when it is, terrible things may happen. As the reader will come to know, this is a tale that brought unforeseen consequences. The ripples of this thread of events were felt in every domain and province. It reached the most hidden and remote nooks of the globe.

INKWELL

AFTERWORD ST.

SCRIVENING ST.

STANZA ST.

TALE ST.

BLACKLETTER LANE

RHYME ROAD

FABLE AVENUE

ALLEGORY ALLEY

RETHORICAL ROAD

COLLOQUY ST.

LONGHAND ST.

ITALICS LANE

ROMAN ROAD

COLOPHON DRIVE

CALLIGRAM ST.

PULP LANE

EPIGRAPH ROAD

VELLUM BOULEVARD

1. GRANDPA DAVEY'S COTTGE
2. MR. TICKERY'S CLOCK FACTORY
3. GRANDPA DAVEY'S BOOKSHOP
4. MONSIEUR PÉPITE'S CHOCOLATE SHOP
5. MR. CAROLING'S WORKSHOP

6. IMOGEN'S COTTAGE
7. IGNATIOUS' COTTAGE
8. PERCIVAL'S COTTAGE
9. THE LIBRARY
10. MR. MCGLUE'S COTTAGE

Because life is made of facts and logic,

Because *two* comes after *one* and before *three*,

And *b* just follows *a* and welcomes *c*,

This story will begin at the beginning,

For that's the way it ought to be.

Who is Florence Ibbot?

One more day. You just have to wait one more day.

Florence kept repeating this to herself that winter morning. Her trip to Inkwell was only twenty-four hours away. But until then, there was school, and all the good and bad things that came along with it. Florence had figured that there were roughly the same amount of pros and cons concerning school. There were things she found mind–catching, like a good algebra quiz, and things she found rather boring, like setting the gym in order after P.E. There were things that were easy, reciting sonnets among them, and things that were, in her own words, gruelling. Dealing with Gideon Green and the Quarrelsome Queens were two perfect examples of that.

But that morning Florence was too excited to mind either the easy or the gruelling things school had to offer. She was just too happy, exactly as she always was before each year's trip to her favourite place. Had she known everything would change during her stay in Inkwell that December, maybe happiness wouldn't have been her feeling of choice. But she didn't know that, so she sat down for her science class, crossed one foot in front of the other and while she sharpened her pencils she thought about her upcoming trip.

She knew she had to calm down and give her attention to school. Not an easy task, but a doable one for sure, especially considering the fact that Florence had acquired a taste for

13

science. This happened because she liked questions, and science answered questions with evidence. The nature of science, she'd come to notice, agreed with her: the need to understand the world and for it to be logical and fair.

Miss Tolworth walked into the classroom with a pile of books in her hands. Her clacking heels announced her entrance before she could utter the usual "Good morning, classroom." Florence's daydreaming about Inkwell popped like a bubble and she snapped back into school-concentration mode.

"Who here can tell me what an ecosystem is?" Miss Tolworth asked, her shrilly voice working as an alarm clock to wake up the students who were still half asleep.

There was silence in the classroom until Florence said, "It's a biological community of organisms that interact between them and with their physical environment."

"EGGHEAD!" Gideon shouted.

Gideon Green's dearest habit was to torture Florence with nasty barbs. He was a cute boy, but his cuteness was hidden underneath his meanness, so truth be told, he looked like a despicable little rascal. He had stubborn curly hair, plump lips and six hundred and seventy-two freckles on his face.

Most bullies tend to operate where adults aren't present, places like unsupervised hallways, remote corners of the playground or the back of the school bus. But Gideon Green didn't mind if teachers, parents or cafeteria chaperones were right there in front of him. He blurted out the yuckiest, prickliest things without caring who was around. In Florence's case, he usually went for GEEK! or LOSER! And on occasions it was a simple and good old-fashioned NERD!

"Silence, Gideon!" Miss Tolworth yelled over the laughter of the entire class. Florence's golden amber eyes turned deep green.

"Her eyes are changing colour again!" a spindly boy whispered.

"That's because she's a weirdo!" Gideon shouted.

The colour of Florence's eyes did in fact follow her spirit. They were gun-metal grey when she was angry, shifted to the brightest golden amber when she felt pleased or happy, coppery flecks appeared when she was thinking too hard and turned deep green when there was sadness in her heart. And when she felt sorrow, it was a sorrow of the most overwhelming kind. Gideon had succeeded in taking away her happiness.

The worst thing was she could never hit back with the same meanness as him. It wasn't like her and she knew no good would come of it. But that didn't mean she was fine with the situation. Oh no. It was the injustice that got to her. No one deserved to be treated like that. Why did he always get away with it? If only there was a trick to become bully-proofed. Florence closed her eyes and said to herself: "One more day. You just have to wait one more day. Then you'll be in Inkwell and far away from Gideon Green."

The laughter had died down and everyone was reading up on ecosystems, nutrient cycling and animal species. Because Florence had already memorized that chapter, her mind began to wander as it sometimes did. Complex as an origami butterfly, Florence sometimes got swamped with questions that cropped up in her head. Questions she thought science still hadn't answered: Are penguins confused about being flightless birds that have to swim? Why do people like horror stories? What are the secrets that have never been revealed? How many treasures have never been found?

That winter morning, having brushed off what sadness was left from Gideon's comment, Florence went running to her teacher at the end of the class with, "Why do wolves sing forlorn ballads to the full moon?"

"Florence, for Heaven's sake, where do you find these questions?"

"I don't find them, they find me."

"Well, then hide from them!" Miss Tolworth said. "Don't let those questions find you."

"Why would I do that?" Florence asked.

"Because you are a child. You can't be brooding about those things. You're only eleven years old. There's no need to worry about serious matters," Miss Tolworth answered.

"But…"

"No buts."

"Still…"

"No buts, no stills, no howevers or yets! Do as I say. Go play with the rest of the class and pay no attention to those things," Miss Tolworth said.

But *those things* meant a great deal to Florence. She wanted to know. So instead of going off to play, she went to the school's library and found a book about wolves. Coppery flecks appeared in her eyes as she looked for the answer.

She discovered that what she thought were forlorn ballads was called howling. That's what wolves did to talk to one another. They did it when the sun went down because they were creatures of the night. She didn't find any evidence connecting the howling to the full moon. Turns out, it was just a way of boosting their sound. Wolves pointed their faces to the night sky and that allowed the howl to carry further.

Now Florence could use the proper word when talking about wolves. They didn't bark or yelp. She figured it was not at all wrong to maybe use the word *bay*, but *howl* was the ideal one.

Florence liked to choose carefully every word she used.

She strove to find the word with the right size for the occasion. *Not too small, not too big. It has to be the word with the perfect fit*, she often thought to herself.

Her favourite one was *pamplemousse*, French for grapefruit. She loved how that exact combination of letters sounded in her English thinking head. It felt like squishing together dozens of bubbles that wouldn't burst.

She'd never forgotten the first word she looked up in the dictionary: *circus*, a travelling company of acrobats, daring animals and loony clowns that gives merry performances in a large tent. Florence thought it was amazing how so many fun things could fit inside one word. And as a matter of fact, the first word she ever uttered was not *mum* or *mamma*. It wasn't *dad* either. The first word out of Florence's mouth was *hyperbole*, and a cheeky look on her face suggested she'd said it with full knowledge of its meaning: exaggerated statements not to be taken literally.

The second and third words out of her mouth came on a day she was very hungry. *Persimmons* and *artichokes*, she said, grabbing one of each from the supermarket aisle. She was colouring a book the day she pronounced her next cluster of words: *flamingo pink*, *myrtle green* and *periwinkle blue*. And the day her parents took her to visit the botanic garden, Florence uttered *yellow primrose* and *autumn catchfly* as she took a whiff of the flowers.

Soon Florence was building sentences like an architect, word upon word, thought upon thought. Now that she was eleven, Florence possessed an unusual verbal extravagance, putting to good use words like *debacle* or *conundrum* or *bodacious*. But this also made her a lonely girl, for not many of the other kids understood what she was saying. She often felt she didn't belong anywhere, like a leafy tree in a cemented playground.

ॐ

Florence closed the book about wolves when she heard the bell ring. She put it back on its shelf and left the library. She crossed the playground where most of the students were still playing as if they hadn't heard the bell and the teachers were trying to herd them back to class. She walked down the hallways till she got to her classroom. Soon everyone else arrived and their ancient history teacher closed the door. Florence sat down and opened her ancient history handbook.

"So my parents gave me all my birthday presents this morning," Tabitha said to Tallulah and Luella as they walked past Florence and made their way to their seats. "I got a piano and a pony, a jewellery box for all my necklaces, because the one I had was already too small, and then a polka-dot skirt and three new lip glosses!"

"Seriously, those are the best presents ever!" Luella said as she sat behind Florence.

"And did I tell you about my birthday party?" Tabitha asked.

Tallulah answered, "We want every detail!"

Florence did her best to tune out their babble. She was known for having a serenity that could calm the most fidgety ferret but it was very hard to be serene around the Quarrelsome Queens. For some unknown law of the universe, Tabitha, Tallulah and Luella were the rulers of the classroom and Florence could not, for the life of her, figure out why. They were conceited and shallow, and loved gossiping. They spoke with irking squeaky voices, bossing everyone around. Their choice of outfits was boringly alike: flared skirt dresses that were always too short or collared shirts with cuffed shorts and knee-high striped socks. They, of course, got a kick out of criticizing anyone who didn't dress exactly like them. And because the Quarrelsome Queens had the habit of biting their

19

nails and all the girls at school were under their ruling, everyone had ragged, uneven fingernails.

∞

When ancient history was over, and so was the non-stop chatter of the Quarrelsome Queens, Florence met with her chess teacher, Mr Rook, and the rest of the chess team to practise for the upcoming championship next semester. Mr Rook was an unbelievably tall man with bulky broad shoulders and a square-shaped head. He spoke with the gravest tone of voice Florence had ever heard and he rarely smiled, but the good thing was he taught the game without overcomplicating what was already quite complicated to begin with. It happened to be the way Florence liked to be taught, with sentences that went straight to the point:

> There are two opponents on opposite sides of a board.
> The board has sixty-four squares.
> The squares are coloured either light or dark.
> Each player has sixteen pieces.
> The bishops are the pieces with pointed hats.
> Knights don't actually look like knights.
> Knights look like horses and can jump like them too.
> The king is the most important piece, but the queen is the most powerful one.
> The goal of the game is to checkmate the opponent's king.
> Checkmate happens when the king is in a position to be captured and cannot escape anywhere.
> In order to do this, one has to master the art of planning.

∞

After a seriously tough and ridiculously long game with Abner, the sharpest chess player in the team, where she had to rack her brains only to lose her king in the end, Florence was sitting on a playground bench. She was reading a book that had nothing to do with chess or ancient history or science. It was just a book she was reading for the fun of it. The best kind of book in her opinion.

"Hey, Florence!" Tabitha shouted.

When she heard Tabitha's raspy voice, Florence raised her head, tucked her hair behind her ear and closed the book. She watched as the Quarrelsome Queens approached her.

"Hey, Florence!" Tabitha shouted again.

"I've heard you. What do you want?" Florence asked politely.

"Today is your turn. I want you to do my homework."

So far they had always gone to other fellow nerds with this request, but never to her. Florence closed her eyes and murmured, "One more day. Inkwell's only a day away."

"What was that?" Tabitha said.

"Nothing," Florence answered.

"Well, you need to do my homework today," Tabitha said.

"No," Florence replied. Her voice was calm. Gideon had already ruined her first half of the morning. She wasn't going to let Tabitha ruin the other half. Florence opened her book and returned to her reading.

"Didn't you hear what Tabitha just told you?" Luella asked as she bit her chipped fingernails.

"I did," Florence answered without taking her eyes off the book. "Didn't you hear my answer was no?"

Tabitha scrunched up her forehead. "Are you saying NO to ME?"

"Yes, I am," Florence answered.

Tabitha's face turned green and it looked like fumes were spouting from her ears. "I'm going to squash you!"

"Yeah! We're going to squash you!" Tallulah and Luella echoed.

"Why would you do that?" Florence asked.

"Because you're saying NO to me and NOBODY says NO to me!" Tabitha said.

"I don't believe that's a valid reason to squash somebody," Florence said.

"But NOBODY says NO to me," Tabitha said.

"That's not true. I just did," Florence said.

"You're looking for trouble, weirdo!" Tabitha said.

"You're looking for someone to think *for* you instead of actually choosing to think for yourself. I won't help you with that," Florence said. She stood up, turned around and walked away from them. She would never give in to their demands, no matter the consequences, for she had decided early on in her life to be *Florence Ibbot* come what may.

Preparations

The way back from school was long. Florence used to loathe every minute of it, that is until the day she discovered that if she paid really close attention, and had her eyes wide open, she could spot the curious things that happened every day on the streets.

She witnessed the seasons change in the flower shop. The florist sold pansies in the winter, tulips in the spring, red valerians in the summer and dahlias that got sprinkled by the autumn rain. On those rainy days of autumn, Florence never used an umbrella. She liked to get wet, splash in the puddles and get mud freckles on her legs.

One day she saw a stray dog that had found his lunch in an alley. Where no one would think an appetizing lunch could be found, this dog had nosed out the crust from a forsaken slice of pizza, a few soggy chips and the remaining bits of fish in a tuna can. She'd also spotted an old man with a mining pick attempting to find gold in the pavement cracks and a very tall lady that was alike, distinguished by the gawkiness of her walk and the skill of crossing the road in four steps.

But that afternoon, Florence barely noticed what was going on in the streets. She could think of nothing but Inkwell. She'd left behind what had happened with Gideon Green and the Quarrelsome Queens because the only thing that mattered was her long-awaited trip.

When she arrived home, there were tea and toast on the kitchen table and a note on the fridge: "Florence, darling, your father and I went to the Odd School to give a lecture. Tea is on the table. We'll be home late."

Florence's parents were very talented, busy mathematicians. They were always giving lectures or marking papers or solving problems. But Florence was fine with that. She considered herself oddly independent so she didn't really mind that they weren't around that often.

Her parents – though hectic academics that usually uttered the classic "I'm sorry, Florence, I have to rush to work" – were both equally delighted and intrigued with their daughter. They believed Florence had peculiar qualities that made her what they in the maths world liked to call *out of the ordinary*: she ate carrot cake when she was sad and had publicly declared her undying love for salted hazelnuts in brown paper bags, warm milk with tons of honey and lumpy mashed potatoes with nutmeg. She hated when her hands got all black and inky after reading the Sunday paper and wasn't too fond of her last name, Ibbot, since it reminded her of the sound people made when they had hiccups.

But that was just scratching the surface. They had found more evidence that supported their *out of the ordinary* theory. Exhibit A: Florence had once devised a kite whose tip would always point in the direction she wanted to go. Exhibit B: She had also fashioned a beanie hat that took away bad dreams and a fabulous folding fan that made her hair smell like jasmine when she swished it. Exhibit C: She had concocted a recipe to bake a velvety vanilla cake and when a person ate only a dainty morsel, they started laughing as if they'd heard the funniest story ever told. The cake was so good her parents could never say no to a slice, even though they knew she would prepare it after doing something naughty and avoid the inconvenience of a scolding. And finally, Exhibit D: Beyond her long black eyelashes there was a glowing wit that could bedazzle the wimpiest sloth.

Florence swapped the tea her mother had left for a cup of warm milk with tons of honey. Then she sat down at the table, took out a notebook and a pencil and wrote down *Travel Packing List*. She slathered a slice of toast with butter and after each bite she jotted down one thing – that way, she would make sure she didn't forget anything. The second piece of toast was spread with apricot jam, and this time Florence made a detailed checklist of all the things she wanted to do once she got to Inkwell. When she finished, there were no other lists pending but she still ate a third slice of toast, this time drizzled with maple syrup.

The afternoon slipped by and soon the sun had disappeared and a few shiny stars were lit in the sky. The day was almost over when the wind began to blow.

As soon as the first swish-swish sound of the wind touched her ears, Florence knew it would happen. It always happened on windy nights. She didn't know why. When she was alone in her bed under her hand-knitted blanket, an itchy feeling loomed in her heart. It was a feeling that told her there was a void in her life. It had nothing to do with the Quarrelsome Queens, nor with Gideon Green. It wasn't something she'd lost either. It was something that had never been there, yet needed to be, like a clock that won't start ticking if it has a missing piece.

As she closed her eyes, the itchy feeling grew bigger and became as pesky as a mosquito. She hated it. It refused to fade despite her many attempts to persuade it otherwise. Since Florence wasn't a whiner (she thought it pointless), she sat up straight in her bed and shouted, "Stop it, you loony itchy feeling! Can't you see I need to get some sleep?" Tomorrow was a big day. She needed to be rested for the journey.

Florence then turned to her foolproof sleeping remedy: binary numbers. That never failed. She dived again into her plump white pillow, took a deep breath, closed her eyes and began counting: *One... One, zero... One, one... One, zero, zero... One, zero, one... One, one, zero... One, one, one... One, zero, zero, zero...zzz...zzz...zzz...*

The Journey to Inkwell

The sky was covered with black clouds and thunder was rumbling in the distance. A rising wind brushed against the trees and made forgotten dead leaves swirl around the lamp posts. Although morning had just begun, it felt like twilight, and smelled like it too. The fading light of the sun had darkened to a deep purple. It felt as if the day had already passed through, only too quickly.

Florence picked the few things she needed for the journey. Every item on her *Travel Packing List* was checked: her cosy wool sweater with really long sleeves, her also notably long fluffy knitted scarf, a hooded poncho, a pair of fringed boots and her Tyrolean hat, which she carried off with the greatest of ease. Except for the boots and the hat, which she always wore on her journey, she put everything else in her green corduroy backpack. She liked to travel light so she never used a suitcase.

Three loud knocks made Florence turn to the door.

"Come in," she said. The door opened and Mrs Ibbot walked into the room.

"We are off to have a breakfast meeting with the dean, darling," her mother said as she put a folder packed with papers in her handbag.

"Oh, I thought you were leaving for Inkwell tomorrow."

"No, today. I've told you three times this week. Four if you count the note I left on your desk."

"I'm sorry, hon, it's just that I'm up to my ears with all this," she said, pointing to the ridiculous amount of papers she'd chucked in her bag. "Are you sure you want to leave now though? It looks like a storm is brewing."

"I'll be fine, Mother. It's just water that will fall from the sky. Besides, I have my umbrella."

"Which you never use," her mother said, half serious, half laughing.

"I will this time, promise. It's just that I'd rather get there wet and sooner than dry and later."

"Very well then. Be very careful with the tricky parts of the journey. Things are very different once you leave the city and head east. Remember the old saying: *once the train crosses the Arcane Bridge, you—*"

"*Have to be ready for the uncanny, the untold and the unimaginable*, I know."

"Good. Say hi to Grandpa for us," her mother said and then pecked her daughter on the forehead.

"I will."

The Farm Fields of Fleeting Feathers

When the train crossed the Arcane Bridge, Florence looked through the window and gazed at the Towering Mountains of the West. The snow-capped peaks twinkled in the distance and foretold a cold winter. Every December, Florence spent a few weeks with her grandfather, Davey, in Inkwell, a small village somewhere southeast of civilization. Tucked away in the hills, Inkwell was a place lost in time. Florence felt at home there. That town, and everyone in it, made her feel like a leafy tree in an evergreen meadow in the folds of a forest.

"Last stop: Old Arcane Station!" a voice announced.

Florence grabbed her backpack and walked down the

corridor of the coach. Only a few passengers were left in the train and they scattered in all directions as soon as the train doors opened. Florence went straight to the Old Arcane Shop, a tiny store near the station that was both a newsstand and a grocery, and bought a bottle of water and a bag of warm hazelnuts. She would have to walk the rest of the trip so she needed to be prepared.

First came the Farm Fields of Fleeting Feathers. Always bathed by the softest glow of the sun, the fields were sowed with fuzzy, yellow feathers that danced in the breeze. Some of the feathers were long and slender; some were shorter but just as lithe. A few of them got detached from the plantations and whirled around, tickling the air.

At first sight it was paradise, but these fields were a bit tricky to cross. The fleeting feathers made the traveller lose track of time. A minute seemed like an hour, a year felt like a day, and the turning of the seasons swept by in seconds. There was no order whatsoever to rule the passage of time. What had been, what was, and what would be happened at once.

The Feather Farmers, who lived nearby and only went into the fields for sowing and harvesting, had taught Florence that the only way to cross these fields without losing herself in time was to set time with the rhythm of her heart. So whenever the fleeting feathers started acting up on her, she would close her eyes and listen within: *baboom baboom…baboom baboom… baboom baboom…* Her heart told her she was where she needed to be: in the present.

Much to her dismay, that's not what happened that winter. As Florence took her first step inside the fields, a steady drizzle began to fall. The light raindrops didn't bother her – she had her umbrella – but with the drizzle came the thunder. It was not rumbling in the distance any more. The crashing noises

29

blasted in after every lightning flash, quashing any other sound in the Farm Fields of Fleeting Feathers.

"I can't hear you, heart!" Florence said, worried of soon being lost in time forever. "Where are you? Please answer me!" She shut her eyes but couldn't hear anything. "No, no, no! This can't be happening!" she cried, but when she opened her eyes, Florence knew not when she was. It was an autumn night and she was a toddler. She suddenly didn't know how to speak and everything around her was gigantic and menacing. In the next blink of her eyes, it was summer time and she was tall and slender. Her body had changed, and so had her thoughts. She thought like a grown-up. "You just have to wait. Thunder can't last for ever." After a minute, or an hour, she couldn't tell, she felt her hands wrinkle and she became aware that she was an elderly woman with all her life behind her. "What's the use of waiting? I'm very tired," she said with a scratchy, wobbly voice.

She squatted on the ground under her umbrella. "Please, Time, stop. Be Now," she said, her voice now thin and high. It was her voice when she had learned to talk. She closed her eyes tight, as if that could help stop time from spinning.

The drizzle became a strong, heavy rain, almost like a tropical shower. Fat raindrops splashed up from newly born puddles in the fields. It wasn't the soft plonking of a fine spray any more but the most forceful downpour she had ever witnessed. It was as if all the rain in the world had decided to fall at once right there. The feathers became completely soaked and flattened.

Florence opened her eyes and found herself in the present. She stepped out from under the umbrella and stood up. Time had stopped whirling. She was once again an eleven-year-old girl on her way to Inkwell on a winter morning.

"What happened? How?" she asked.

It was an old Feather Farmer who was nearing the fields that gave her the answer. "The wet feathers, honey," he said. "When a downpour hits these fields, the feathers lose their magic. A minute doesn't seem like an hour. A minute is a minute. A year no longer feels like a day. A year lasts three hundred and sixty-five days. The turning of the seasons doesn't sweep by in a wink. The turning of the seasons is every three months. Only when the feathers are soaking wet–"

"There exists in the field a perfect order to rule time," Florence said.

"Exactly. Now, get out of here before these feathers dry!" And Florence did as the farmer said.

The Pathway of Pedantic Plum Trees

The skies had cleared, the storm was long gone and so were the Farm Fields of Fleeting Feathers. The sun now shone in the Pathway of Pedantic Plum Trees. Florence walked quickly, trying not to attract too much attention, but as it happened every time, the trees spotted her at once. There was no way to avoid them, shush them or even lull them down.

"Our plums are rich in so many vitamins!" a tall plum tree shouted out.

"And not only that," another plum tree said, "just imagine all the things you can do with our fruit: pies, jams, jellies, smoothies, chutneys, crumbles, the list is endless, I'll tell you that."

"Well, of course! And if that wasn't enough, the plum is a natural remedy. It settles the stomach like no other fruit," the tall plum tree added.

The Pedantic Plum Trees' broadcast had begun. Florence wished there was another road she could take to get to Inkwell, but the pathway was surrounded by the Towering Mountains of the North to one side and the Towering Mountains of the South to the other. She had no choice but to put up with the bragging, obnoxious trees. She sighed and kept walking without making any comments.

"You can never get bored with us, you know. We come in every colour: red plums, blue–black plums, yellow plums, and the ones I like the most, the purple ones!" a tree with purple plums said as he saw her approaching.

"What about silver plums?" Florence didn't resist the temptation to ask.

"Well, erm, there are no silver plums, but then again, there is no other fruit that comes in that colour!" the purple plum tree answered.

"Don't you think you are being a tad too boastful?"

"Nonsense!"

"It may play to your advantage to be less arrogant."

"We aren't arrogant. We just have a good opinion of ourselves."

"I'm not saying plums aren't good. I really like them, but if you eat apples, for example, you don't have to visit the doctor that often, and bananas have freckles and give you lots of energy."

The purple plum tree's cocky smile quickly faded into a frown.

"Oranges," Florence continued, "look good on any breakfast table and grapes are so much fun to eat one right after the other *plop-plop-plop-plop*, don't you think?"

The purple plum tree's branches cramped and his leaves rattled. The only reaction at his disposal was to scowl at the young girl standing in front of him and blurt out, "That may very well be the case, but we are still better. Can't you tell?"

Florence scratched her head. She was getting a bit tired of insisting on this fruitless debate. These trees were not only arrogant, they were stubborn. They weren't going to change their minds in spite of her good arguments to do so. As she left the pathway, she could hear the trees still bragging behind her.

"We make the most delicate flowers!"

"And even if our fruit goes dry, it's still delicious… The one and only, the prune, what a treat!"

The Great Grumbling Grassland

When the Pathway of Pedantic Plum Trees ended, the Great Grumbling Grassland began. The land was covered with long, shaggy grasses, sedges and vines. In there, nothing was tamed. All the plants grew freely without the care of humans. No rules could be broken because there were no rules to break.

It was rather difficult to range over the jungly grassland, but Florence had done this many times so she knew exactly which was the best way to do it. She used a thick blade of grass as a skateboard and soared down the grassland hills. She loved the speed, being able to steer her direction by shifting her body like a wave from side to side. Her hair swung wildly as she skated past the high-rise green leaves of grass.

Halfway through the crossing, she heard them. It was loud and impossible to miss. Florence pressed down on the back tail of the blade and made a sharp stop. She ran towards the sound.

Within the Great Grumbling Grassland there lived a tribe of wombats who played the bongos. Their music had a tumbling rhythm that travelled through the ground and the air. As she got closer, the sound grew louder, and when they saw her arrive, the wombats waved at her and started playing even louder.

"Florence! Welcome back!" one of them said.

"It's good to be back!" Florence said as she took off her fringe boots and started dancing barefoot, feeling the earth between her toes. The rumbling grew stronger.

RUM PA PA PUMP!

RUM PA PA PUMP!

POOM POOM POOM!

RUM PA PA PUMP!

RUM PA PA PUMP!

POOM POOM POOM!

They were soon joined by every creature that lived in the grassland, from bumblebees to frogs to monkeys and toucans. They all had their signature dance moves. The loud, upbeat sound of the drums pounding together stirred up the wind while everyone jumped, stamped the ground and swung their arms around.

"These drums," Florence shouted as she danced, "what is it about them? They make the best music I've ever heard!"

"Oh, you can do a whole lot more with these drums than just play music," one of the wombats said.

"What do you mean?" Florence asked.

"These are really special instruments," another wombat said. "I guess the exact word would be *powerful.*"

"Well, what can you do with them?"

"One cannot put it into words," the first wombat said, "one has to see it in action. You'll one day see what we mean."

With that last comment lingering in her head, Florence got ready to continue on. She knew, even though she loved to dance, that she couldn't stay long. This was only a stop on her journey to Inkwell.

"Leaving already?" a wombat next to her said as she was putting on her fringe boots.

"I have to, otherwise I won't get to Inkwell before sunset. I'll see you on my way back!"

"We'll be waiting for you with new POOM POOMS and RUM PA PA PUMPS!"

"Counting on it!"

The Riveting River Valley

Florence followed the river course for a little over an hour. She'd left the Great Grumbling Grassland filled with pizzazz but the long walk had tired her out, so as she was nearing the valley she made a quick stop. She knelt by the river. The frothy current swept by as she sank her hands into it. The water was cold but refreshing and it gave her what she needed to pick up her journey.

After a mile or so, Florence caught sight of the valley. She smiled, as did most of the travellers who got to this place. A person had to be seriously unhappy not to enjoy a stay here. Why? Because the Riveting River Valley was the place where all the game inventors lived. Games for every taste were invented there. Memory games, logic games, dancing games and singing ones. Games played with cards or boards or dice. From the hardest strategy games to the coolest arcade games, they were all created in this valley.

The game inventors dressed in trousers and red argyle sweaters with matching socks. They carried pencils tucked behind their ears and they all had fine, neatly clipped moustaches that took the shape of a thin line as if drawn with a felt-tip pen. None of them had wrinkles on their faces because they knew how to have fun with their job, which was easy since playing was the most essential part of their workday.

As soon as Florence made it to the valley, she spotted one of her favourite inventors. His name was Melvin and his red argyle sweater was too tight for his big round belly. His speciality was riddles. Florence saw him seated on a log near one of the game factories, eating a glazed doughnut.

"Do you have a riddle for me today, Melvin?"

"Florence! How nice to see you again!"

"It's nice to see you again too, Melvin."

"Are you on your way to Inkwell?"

"I am."

"Happy you're going to see your granddad again?"

"Very."

"Good trip so far?"

"So far. Every bit has its charms, so to speak. Though as usual, I'm not particularly looking forward to the last bit."

"Yeah, those woods. You are a brave little soul going in there all alone."

"It's the only way to get to Inkwell. There's no way around it," Florence said as she watched Melvin take a huge bite of the doughnut.

"Oh, where are my manners?" Melvin said with his mouth full. "Would you like a doughnut?" He picked up a carton that had a chocolate-frosted doughnut and a custard-filled doughnut.

"I'm quite hungry really." She picked the custard one. Then she sat beside him, took off her Tyrolean hat and set her green corduroy backpack on the ground.

"So you said you were in need of a riddle, huh?"

"I could use one, yes."

"Let's see…" Melvin pondered as he ate the last bit of his doughnut and licked his fingers. "I'll think of one that will make you squeeze your brains. You'll have to cerebrate and ruminate and…"

"Don't make it too hard," Florence said as she took a bite of her custard-filled doughnut. "But don't go too easy on me either."

Melvin grabbed the pencil that was behind his ear and a notepad that was in his back pocket. He started writing. He stopped. He thought for a few seconds. He chewed the pink rubber on the tip of the pencil. He wrote some more. He paused again. He erased the last bit he had written. He wrote a new bit. And a bit more after that. He re-read what he'd just written, he double-checked everything and then handed the piece of paper over to Florence.

"It's a poem," she said.

"It's a poem about a word. And *in* the poem that word hides as well. Can you guess what word it is?"

"Let's see if I can." Florence looked at the piece of paper. The poem read:

> Perhaps Wow! will be yapped when this riddle's figured out,
> Aha! too is a word that will bring this rub about;
> Long ago an old nun celebrated that she had one,
> I am proud that my mum and my dad also snatched one;
> None there are in Amsterdam, nor in Sydney or Japan,
> Dread no more for in Neuquén hides another one again;
> Refer too will bring you near to the thing you wish to hear,
> On the dot it comes at noon and then falls into a swoon;
> Mary doesn't, nor does Lana, but it does belong to Hannah.
> Every eye that likes to peep suffers from it, yes indeed!
> So in the end or the beginning, in a good deed you'll find
> the meaning.

"How dreadfully clever you are, Melvin," Florence said, looking at the poem.

"So do you have the answer?" Melvin asked.

"No…not yet anyway. But I never ever give in or up, so just give me a moment here, will you?"

She read it again, slowly, hefting every word and snooping into every sentence, hunting all the clues to find the word that was hidden in there. She searched like a detective with a magnifying glass. She cerebrated and ruminated and squeezed her brains just as Melvin had predicted she would. And that's how she found the answer.

Raising an eyebrow, she looked at Melvin. Then she leaned and whispered the answer in his ear.

"Exactly so, Miss Florence Ibbot, exactly so!"

Florence smiled proudly and went on to say, "It reads the same backward as forward. From right to left, from left to right, this sneaky word now comes to sight." She grabbed his pencil and circled the first letter of every line. Therein lay the answer.

"You do know your words, huh?" Melvin said.

"What can I say, I love me a good quirky word."

"Well, good job. Congratulations!" he cheered. "I look forward to seeing you soon and cooking up another riddle for you."

"Me too, Melvin." She thanked him for the riddle and the doughnut. She put on her Tyrolean hat, picked up her green corduroy backpack, said a fond goodbye and journeyed on.

The Wood of Whispering Weeping Willows

As Florence had told Melvin, the hardest part of the road to Inkwell was crossing the Wood of Whispering Weeping Willows. Within the limits of this wood, laughter did not exist. The trees in there lived in eternal sorrow. They carried sadness in their branches, their sap was dark and bitter, and

their leaves drooped with melancholy.

The thick air made it difficult for Florence to see clearly and the sorrow of the weeping willows clung to every inch of her skin. She grabbed a branch and used it as a walking stick to probe the ground. She walked as fast as she could.

Florence could hear the weeping willows whisper and it was only unhappy words. Some of their voices were hollow, others were coarse, and when fused together, it was like hearing a hideous moan that bled into the wood. She had once tried stuffing cotton balls in her ears to cushion the whispering, but it hadn't worked. It wasn't enough of a barrier. The sadness was not only heard but felt and seen and smelled everywhere in the woods.

The ground was moist from all the tears the trees had shed. A curling mist hovered above quicksand and rotten deadfall. There were patches of scummy water, slime-coated rocks, and too many shadows. "Shut up, shut up, shut up!" Florence couldn't help but cry to the willows. When they didn't listen, she told herself, "Come on, Florence, walk faster. We need to get out of this woodland!"

She dodged the quicksand, the slippery rocks and the shadows, but that wasn't the hardest part for her. She had to fight not to let grief reach her the way it had reached the deep roots of the willows. It was almost as if happy thoughts refused to come to such a place.

There was only one thing she could do: remember why she was there. She thought of Inkwell. The journey's end was all that mattered. She held on to that, awfully tight, as if that thought was the most precious possession she'd ever owned. But it wasn't enough. She had to find something more powerful to make it out of there, something that would shut those trees up. And then an idea popped into her head: the wombats of the

Great Grumbling Grassland. She started playing their song in her head.

RUM PA PA PUMP!

RUM PA PA PUMP!

POOM POOM POOM!

"Louder," Florence said. "It has to be louder! You can do better than this."

RUM PA PA PUMP!

RUM PA PA PUMP!

It seemed to be working. The weeping willows' sad voices were becoming fainter.

POOM POOM POOM!

RUM PA PA PUMP!

RUM PA PA PUMP!

"Come on, Florence, LOUDER!" she shouted as she kept walking forward.

RUM PA PA PUMP!

RUM PA PA PUMP!

POOM POOM POOM!

POOM POOM POOM!

And it worked, if only to make it out of the woods as untouched by sadness as possible.

∞

At last, Florence reached her destination: Inkwell. A sleepy, ancient limestone village sprinkled with cottages with thatched roofs, lilies and daffodils on the windows, and woolly sheep roaming the gardens. Right in the middle of town, there was a main square with a maple tree and a water well that hadn't been used for years.

Grandpa Davey was the owner of the oldest bookshop in the village. In there, all the classics and other rare books were always awaiting new readers. Florence thought it was the coolest shop in the world.

"Grandpa!" Florence shouted as soon as she saw him.

"My dear! Welcome!" Grandpa Davey said.

The itinerary was the same as the year before, and the year before that and the one before that one. Grandpa Davey welcomed her at the wrought-iron gateway of his cottage, but they didn't go into the house. They went straight to the old bookshop.

There was a bell on the entrance door that greeted them with a tinkle as they walked inside. Florence took off her Tyrolean hat, tossed her green corduroy backpack on the floor and rushed to the shelves in the hopes of finding her next book. She was so anxious she could barely finish reading one title before moving on to the next.

To her delight, she found too many good options. She narrowed it down to three: an old edition of a classic, a mystery novel and a memoir of a wise and daring king. Grandpa Davey put the books in a bag and together they made their way back to the cottage.

In her bedroom at Grandpa Davey's cottage, there was a set of bookshelves that gladly received its new tenants. Although not for long. Florence was not one to let books gather dust on the shelves. She believed books were meant to be read, and straight away. Stories got melancholic if they were cast aside and forgotten. Characters could lose brightness and colour, like an old photograph, if one waited too long to start reading.

Ben

Florence made him with a piece of carton, watercolours, a black felt-tip pen and a pair of scissors. He was a reminder. She named him Ben, short for Benjamin, since he was the smallest she'd ever made so far. She always crafted a new one for every book she started reading, either matching the colour of the cover or the theme of the novel. But this time, Florence hadn't chosen a book yet. Still doubting if she should go for the old classic, the mystery novel or the memoir of a wise and daring king, Florence decided to create Ben anyway.

Every other time she'd made a bookmark, she'd worked in silence, but that morning two lonely lines of a poem kept dancing in her head. She'd always liked those two lines and so she sang them while making her bookmark.

Every morn and every night
Some are born to sweet delight.

Florence cut the carton with flowing movements. Once she had the shape, she traced the bookmark's features. He looked like a chubby kidney bean. Florence drew him two eyes, a little mouth, and a big pleated cap like the ones worn by the engine drivers of old trains. Because she hadn't decided on the book, she picked the colours and shape of the bookmark at random. Well, not entirely at random. She did have a liking both for baked beans and train rides. Then came the water-colour washes. A little bit of blue and violet, some yellow over

here and a soft orange glow over there, all blending together nicely.

When she finished her bookmark, she tidied up her desk and went outside to help Grandpa Davey gather some leeks and potatoes from the vegetable garden to make a soup for lunch.

❧

When Florence closed the door and left the room, Ben opened his eyes. He stood up and looked around. All was quiet. He walked to the edge of the desk and sat there. He softly rested his hands on his knees and took a deep breath. He sighed and sponged up his first few moments in the world.

"So this is life…" he murmured. "Not bad. Not bad at all." He turned to his left and gazed up at the shelves lined with books. "There they are!" Although he was still murmuring, the room was so silent his voice echoed all around. "Oh, I want to see the inside of a book. Which one will it be? I hope it's not a boring one, though by the selection on those shelves, it looks like my creator would never choose a dull book. Are there dull books? I guess there must be. I'm sure I'll get a good one though, one that draws you in with the first chapter, or the first sentence, a page-turner as they say. But I'm not one to complain. I'll be fine with whatever I get."

He heard noises. Someone was approaching. He went back to the exact place where he'd woken up and stayed stiff as a board.

The door of the room opened and someone walked inside. "It has to be her," Ben thought. He opened one eye, only a fraction. He wanted to see his creator. The first thing he saw were her fringe boots. Then came the really long sleeves of her fluffy sweater and the locks of her bouncy brown hair. As she turned towards the wardrobe, Ben caught a glimpse of her bright golden amber eyes.

"Florence!" someone called from the garden.

"I'll be right there, Grandpa!" Florence answered, "I'm just getting my gloves and scarf. It's freezing outside!" Ben saw that Florence grabbed her things and ran out of the room. He heard her steps going down the stairs. His heart was pounding out of his chest. Too many things in so little a span of time.

℘

Grandpa Davey and Florence came into the kitchen with two baskets full of leeks, potatoes and some chives Florence had spotted in a corner of the vegetable garden and had thought would make a nice addition to the soup. The kitchen was warm. Inside the wood-fired oven, a big round loaf of bread was rising.

Florence took off her gloves and scarf and tossed them on a chair. Grandpa Davey left his jacket and woolly vest on. No matter if it was freezing cold or boiling hot, Grandpa Davey always wore the tweed jackets and sweater vests that Grandma Winifred had made for him. These old-fashioned outfits fitted perfectly with his round face, his plump cheeks that almost hid his button nose, his bright blue eyes, and his cotton candy-like white beard.

"I think I'll go visit Hephy this afternoon," Florence said.

"You should probably wait a day or two. It's been snowing non-stop and the road to Scriptoria Hill is blocked."

"Oh…"

"I bet you really want to see her."

"Yep. I really do. I guess I'll have to wait."

"Only a few days. The skies will clear soon."

Grandpa Davey cleaned and chopped the leeks. Florence washed, peeled and cut up the potatoes into cubes. Grandpa Davey heated some olive oil in a pan and added the leeks and a minced clove of garlic. When everything was soft, Florence added the potatoes and some vegetable stock. They liked to cook together. They worked in a neat manner, cleaning up as they went along so the kitchen was never in too much of a mess. While they waited for the potatoes to get tender, they set the table and discussed the wonders of culinary science.

"A lot of cooking," Grandpa Davey said, "is essentially a series of chemical reactions."

"Uh-huh," Florence agreed. "It's all a matter of what we can find in this kitchen and how that stuff changes when we jumble it together, right?"

"Exactly, my dear," Grandpa Davey answered. "Like the very same bread we have in the oven right now. The yeast is making the dough rise and rise and rise."

"Or eggs! You can heat them, beat them or mix them and get a fried egg, an omelette or a flan."

"Besides, knowing about kitchen chemistry can help you avoid disasters, like that time when I–"

"Grandpa?" Florence said, looking at the bubbling pan on the stove.

"Yes, my dear?"

"I think the soup is ready." Florence pointed to the saucepan. Soup bubbles were bursting and spilling all over the place.

"Oh my! Speaking of cooking chemistry!" Grandpa Davey got up and turned the stove off.

Florence whizzed the soup with a hand blender until the mix was perfectly smooth. She tossed in a smidgen of salt and pepper and poured the soup into a big ceramic bowl with two handles. She sprinkled some finely chopped chives on top and carried the bowl to the table. Grandpa Davey opened the oven and smelled the baked bread. He took the loaf out and placed it on a wooden board.

"This bread is ready to be spread with butter," he said.

"Or dipped into the soup," Florence suggested.

As she was about to plunge the knife into the bread to cut a few slices, Grandpa Davey yelled, "NO!" And Florence stopped mid-air. Grandpa Davey then said, "Knives are for steaks. They do not go well with bread, any loaf will tell you that. Rip a chunk with your hands!"

"Really? Hands?" Florence asked.

"It will have a better taste, I promise you. The steel takes all the flavour away. The hands, as long as they are clean, keep the original taste."

They both sat at the kitchen table and Florence tore a piece of bread with her hands and tried it. Her grandfather was right. It did taste better. With a long copper ladle, she poured some leek and potato soup into two smaller bowls. She handed one to Grandpa Davey and put the other one in front of her.

"Ooh! Scorching!" Grandpa Davey said. He blew upon a new spoonful and had another try. "Mmhhh, there we go, much better."

"Scrumptious and mouth-watering and every other adjective that praises food!" Florence said, sipping spoonful after spoonful of soup without noticing its temperature.

"It has a particular taste," Grandpa Davey said, savouring the soup as if it were wine.

"It's the chives."

"The chives! Great touch!"

Not a word flew in the kitchen while they ate their lunch. As the bowls were starting to get empty and Grandpa Davey was using a piece of bread to wipe up the last bit of soup from his bowl, he asked Florence, "So, have you chosen a book yet?"

"No, not yet. I still can't decide."

"I could help you with your decision, but I won't. I believe each one must choose their own reading. There's always the perfect book for the perfect time, and no one can decide that but the person who will read it."

"I know, Grandpa. I'll make my decision soon. You know I believe books are meant to be read straight away."

A Curious Encounter

As he waited for Florence to start reading a new book, Ben spent his time on her desk, near a coaster made of cork that looked annoyed when tea drops spilled and got him stained, and a blue ceramic pot with pencils and crayons.

Ben knew that a good bookmark had to be patient – it was a job that required tons of patience – so he tried to control himself since his level of nervousness was at its highest. Since Florence wasn't in the room, he walked hastily, bouncing like a bunny, to one of the edges of the desk and then to the other. His neck and forehead were sweaty. He took off his hat and fanned himself. He rubbed his hands and said in a slow voice, "Breathe, breeeeathe, you'll do a good job."

Despite his worry, Ben was very well prepared to do his job. He had felt how life was poured into him with every stroke of the brush, every drop of paint and every cut of the scissors on the carton. He knew he was special, the first of Florence's bookmarks to come to life. And he also knew she didn't know that yet.

He liked Florence's bedroom. It smelled like cinnamon, old books and newly thought sonnets. There was a long mirror resting against one of the walls and a pair of chalky white Oxford shoes with really long shoelaces that created figures on the oak wood floor.

In front of the desk there was a big window and as the

afternoon set in, a warm orangey light filled the room. Ben stood at the edge of the desk and, through the panes, he got a glimpse of the garden: there was a vegetable garden, a penny-farthing bike, and an ash tree that had already lost most of its leaves and was waiting for more snow that was due to arrive any day now.

Ben also spotted two sheep strolling along Grandpa Davey's yard, eating grass and looking solemnly amused. Since he didn't know their names, or if they had been named at all, he baptized them Zelda and Zelia, because those names fitted; the two sheep resembled a couple of elegant old lady friends having tea all day long.

ॐ

On his first night, Ben tried to sleep but couldn't. He tossed and turned. Everything was still and silent. Florence was sound asleep. Ben's eyes, on the contrary, were wide open. He lay on the desk, resting his head on a little white rubber that served as a pillow.

Out of the corner of his eyes, he saw something moving in the darkness on the other side of the desk. He got up, rubbed his eyes and took another look. "What is that?" he thought. His curious side wanted to know what was out there. His fearful side also wanted to know what it was. He wasn't going to sleep peacefully knowing that something was out there. So, with a faint voice, partly because he didn't want to wake up Florence and partly because he was scared out of his wits, he whispered, "Is someone there?"

There was no answer but Ben could see that something was indeed making its way to the end of the desk and towards the bookshelves.

"H-h-hello," Ben stuttered. "Who's there? Who are you?"

Complete and utter silence. But whoever it was had stopped moving and looked to where the voice was coming from.

Ben took a deep breath and walked forward. The figure in the darkness had resumed his travelling, creeping through the desk making tiny waves as he moved along. He had a long, slender, soft body and he didn't move too quickly. Ben hurried and stopped in front of him.

"Who are you?" Ben asked, his voice still holding a hint of a quiver.

"I'm Barnaby."

Ben saw the little creature that was before him. He was not *that* scary. Sure, he had kind of a slimy body and he looked a bit like a squirrel's tail, but all that aside, he seemed to be harmless. A bit relieved, Ben said, "Hi there, Barnaby, I'm Ben, the bookmark."

"Well," Barnaby said politely, "if we are doing formal introductions, then I guess I should introduce myself again. Hello, I'm Barnaby, the bookworm. Nice to meet you!"

"BOOKWORM?"

"Yes, a bookworm. You've never heard of bookworms before?"

"Um… Yes, yes I have."

Ben knew about bookworms all right. They were ravenous creatures that gnawed at books like a dog at his bone and injured them beyond repair. Ben was stunned. He made an effort to say something and this was all that came out of his mouth, "But…but you…you EAT books!"

"Technically, I work chiefly on the pages and the leather binders, and I also eat the paste of the bindings, but yes, you could say I eat books," Barnaby said. "I'm on my way to those bookshelves for my midnight snack. I've never been there before, but I was told I would find some tasty, fine books in there!" It sounded as if Barnaby's mouth was now watering.

Ben raised his right hand and stopped him. "NO! You can't do that! You riddle the books with holes! That's wrong!"

"But they are small holes," Barnaby said in his defence.

"That doesn't make it any better! You're still destroying books. That's a serious crime."

"But I always try to find old, unused books," Barnaby said, portraying an appealingly innocent gaze.

"Every book is special, it doesn't matter if it's old or new. And there's no such thing as an unused book. There may be bad book owners, but that's not the book's fault."

"You don't understand, we bookworms are always hungry! I never lose my appetite! EVER! What am I to do if I can't eat books?"

"I'm sorry but I can't let you through."

"But what can I do? I can't change. I'm a bookworm. I eat books. I can't help it!"

"I don't appreciate when people use the phrase '*I can't help it!*' What does that mean? Of course you can help it. It's a matter of choice. You have to decide what you think is more important." Ben was quite mad but as he saw Barnaby's remorse, he quickly picked a sweeter tone of voice. "And you *can* change. I will help you if you want."

"How could you possibly help me?"

"For your information," Ben said, "I know a lot of things, more than you can imagine."

"Oh, yeah. Like what?"

"Like red and white make pink, evergreen trees don't lose their leaves in the winter and a crane is both a bird and a machine to move heavy objects."

"Everybody knows that."

"OK. How about this? Two is the first prime number, a porcupine can fight off a pride of lions, a sestina is a poem that has thirty-nine lines, iron is the fourth most common element in the Earth's crust, and coffee beans aren't beans, they're fruit pits. On that note, pomology is the science of fruit-growing."

"Huh, how come you know so much stuff?"

"I just do. That's how bookmarks are. We're born well-read and wise on several matters of the world."

"In that case, I'm sorry about my previous comment. I didn't mean to offend you. It's just that I really don't see how you can help me."

"That's OK. Let's see… Have you ever tried a different diet?"

"No, not really."

"How about if I found you something to replace the books?"

Barnaby took a moment to consider the proposal. "That could work," he finally said, "but it would have to be a dish as yummy as books. Only then would I consider it."

"Deal."

Ben thought for a while. He walked in circles with his arms clasped behind his back. Barnaby looked at him and began to think too.

"I've got it!" Ben snapped.

"You do?"

"I think so, yes. Listen to this: gossip magazines and scandalous tabloids," Ben said, but Barnaby looked confused. "Don't you see? These things spread slander and rumours. They don't serve any good purpose. They have nothing but written lies in them," Ben said. "You would actually be doing the world a huge favour."

A grin popped up on Barnaby's face, so Ben carried on mapping out his plan.

"If you find a tabloid printing factory, you could stop travelling from book to book. You could settle there and binge on that delightful gossip non-stop."

"Are you sure about this?"

"Positive."

"That sounds too good to be true."

"I'm not lying. I never lie."

"Well then, we should tell Bruno," Barnaby said, smacking his lips.

"Bruno? Who's Bruno?"

"He's my best friend, and a fellow bookworm. He's the greatest glutton. He can eat an entire encyclopaedia in one sitting. He's famous, I'll have you know," Barnaby said.

"You don't say," Ben mumbled, thinking how awful that was, but understanding what an accomplishment it would be in the bookworm world.

"He's already up there. See? Look, over there, on *The Hunchback of Notre Dame*," Barnaby said, looking up to the bookshelves.

Ben looked up and saw Bruno, a bulky bookworm that was holding on to the binder of the book like a spider monkey.

"Hey, Bruno!" Barnaby said. "Come down here!"

Bruno frowned. Looking slightly ticked off, probably because he was being forced to interrupt his banquet, he made his way down the bookshelves. Barnaby then explained to him what Ben had told him.

"Then what are we going to eat?" Bruno asked, no doubt picturing a future of starvation. So Barnaby and Ben told him all about the new gossip magazine diet.

"Not too shabby for me. And we wouldn't have to move

around any more looking for books and libraries?" Bruno asked, no doubt picturing a future of eternal bliss.

"Nope," Barnaby and Ben answered at the same time.

"OK, I'm in," Bruno said. "Let's do it."

Ben watched as Barnaby and Bruno slithered smoothly towards their new abode. Then he turned around to look at the bookshelves. Florence's books were safe now. He had to admit he was quite proud of himself.

The night was again perfectly quiet. Florence had slept through the entire episode. Ben was still staring at the crowded shelves. So many books lived there. He had heard about most of them: the one about a little prince; the one where a spider and a pig became friends in a farm; the one about knotty lives of an orphan and his friend, a skilful pickpocket. The list was endless. All he had to do was wait until Florence decided into which new story she wanted to enter.

But as it turned out, Ben didn't have much time, for the moon was changing. A waning half-moon was drawing near, and though he was unaware of it yet, that meant rambunctious events were bound to unfold.

The Imp

The decision was made. Ben was granted entrance to *The Adventures of Tom Sawyer*. He was glad that of the three options Florence had found in the bookshop, she'd picked the old edition of what it was known to be a classic. Pretty much the perfect choice for a bookmark's debut.

He snuggled between the cover and the introduction. The pages had that particular frosty pinecone smell that many used books have. The words were anxious to be read. Ben could almost feel them shake.

On the first night, he introduced himself. He explained to the words that he was a bookmark and that he would be living there with them, making sure Florence knew where she'd stopped reading. On the second night, since they were all better acquainted, he told them all about his dream of one day learning how to play the ukelele and how he liked animal names that began with the letter o, so he fantasized about having a farm with ostriches, otters, owls and orangutans and a pond full of octopuses, orcas and oysters.

"What else would you like to do?" the word *Dream* asked Ben.

"Well, if I ever have the time, I long to be the skipper of a fishing boat, stand behind the tiller and have an adventure at sea!" Ben said.

"What else? What else?" *Brimming* asked.

"Um, let's see… I think I might have the skills to be good dominoes player, but I'm not so sure," Ben answered.

"I think you'd make a fine dominoes player, but I really like you as our bookmark too," *Waver* said.

"You don't have to worry, *Waver*, I'll always be a bookmark. It's my reason to be. And my work here has only just begun. I'm not going anywhere."

On the third night, Ben was about to open up another chitchat when he heard someone weeping. He looked around and discovered the word *I* hunched up on her line of the page.

"Are you alright there?" Ben asked her. "Why are you crying?"

"It's just that I'm so small compared to her." *I* pointed to the word *Handkerchief.*

"There's no need to cry. Size isn't everything, you know," Ben said.

"But she's so long and curvy," *I* said. "Look at me. I'm all skinny and short. I fill so little space on this page."

"But you're really important," Ben said.

"I am?" *I* said, sobbing.

"You wouldn't have been able to ask that question if you didn't exist," Ben said.

"What about me?" *Vanity* asked.

"You too, *Vanity*, you all have your purpose." Ben looked at the words around him. "You're all meaningful."

"As in full of meaning?" *Backward* asked.

"Let's put it this way: thanks to you, human beings can think and talk and understand the world around them. Don't you think that's kind of important?"

The words nodded.

"People can't say what they are feeling without you. No one would be able to make a promise or argue their point or congratulate someone on doing a good job. No one ever told you this before?"

"No, sir," *Aunt* said. "We were just thrown here one day by an old, ghastly machine that made lots of noises."

"Well, you must never forget this then: you are the carriers of meaning," Ben said.

"Where do we have to carry it?" *Boy* asked.

"No, no, you don't have to take it anywhere. It's yours. You own it."

"Awesome. I don't think I've ever owned anything before. My meaning is mine. Ha!" *Boy* said.

"And if that wasn't enough, once you are all together in a sentence, you get weaved with these guys" – Ben pointed to the punctuation signs – "to create rhythm and sense."

"Indeed!" the exclamation point exclaimed.

"But what does that mean?" the question mark asked, puzzled and wavy.

"It means the stop separates, the comma pauses and the colon clarifies," *Teacher* explained.

"So we should always remember our meaning and bear it with pride," *Final* said because she needed to have the last word of the conversation.

ॐ

Life was good and neat and simple. As Florence read her book, Ben went from page 1 to page 16 to page 29 to page 42 to page 55. Every time he landed on a new page, he met new words and they got him up to speed with the part of the story he had skipped.

Everything was as it should be. It had only been a few days since he'd gone into *The Adventures of Tom Sawyer* but the words already looked up to him. Ben couldn't have asked for anything better.

The fourth night in the book was a quiet winter night. It showed no signs of tragedy in its skies. Still from that moment forward, nothing would ever be the same. As a waning half-moon started to crawl up the sky, an evil spark lit up inside Ben.

At first it was nothing but a tickle, but then the tickle became a twinge and when the twinge faded and Ben thought everything had passed, there came a wave of cold shivers that made Ben feel there was a hurricane inside him.

He did his best to fight it, but this was a force much stronger than him. It had a life of its own and it was controlling every inch of his body from within, making him squiggle like a loony worm. He could feel his head stir and his hands swell. Something horrendous was boiling up inside him. Ben kept trying to resist it but the spark kept growing.

He screamed "NO!" and "STOP!" and "PLEASE!" but whatever it was that was taking over him did not heed his begging.

When he couldn't take it any more, he closed his eyes and surrendered to it. The words on the page witnessed how Ben's gentle eyes were swapped for a treacherous wild look. Two mushroom-like ears popped up on top of his head. A row of spikes sprung on his back and a leathery, thick tail on his bottom. His skin turned greenish black and was covered with warts that reeked of steamed Brussels sprouts.

The horrible creature opened his eyes. The words were flooded with dread, but they couldn't take their attention off of him. He grinned, displaying sharp stick-out teeth and a long, slimy tongue. He put on rubber flip-flops and shook his whole body to brush off any grain of kindness left. He then surveyed his surroundings.

"What's just happened? Where's Ben? Who's that awful

55

abominable beast?" the word *Questions* whispered.

"I'm not sure I know," *Doubt* answered.

"Whatever it is, I bet no sergeant, lieutenant or captain would want to face him in battle," *Grave* said.

"That's not a beast! That's an imp!" the word *Smart* said and choked back a shriek.

"I'm scared!" *Fearful* said.

"So am I," *Same* concurred.

"Who will come to our rescue?" *Help* asked and then the word *Moan* began to whimper.

"Shhhhh!" It was *Hush* who shushed them all.

The imp saw the look of horror on the words. He smirked and said:

> *Pox, the Imp… That is my name,*
> *I am the one that words can't tame.*
> *My powers go beyond what you dare think,*
> *With one swift blow I can erase all ink.*
> *And with this olden spell you will forget*
> *That I was ever here and that we've met.*

Then he walked to the edge of the book, leaving a trail of deadly fog behind him. He squatted down, took a little black pencil from behind his mushroom-like ear, and wrote something on the left margin of the page. None of the words could make out what it was and they didn't dare move an inch to peep. The imp then stood up, raised one eyebrow and… POOOF! He vanished from page 55.

∓

The next morning, Florence walked into her bedroom with a cup of hot cocoa in her hand. She always had hot cocoa in the morning, because otherwise the day didn't start properly. She sat down at the desk, her legs hanging since the chair was too high for an eleven-year-old girl. She hooked Ben with her index finger and opened the book.

When Florence glanced over the first few sentences, she realized that this was not where she had stopped reading. The bookmark was many chapters ahead in the story.

"Hmm, that's weird," she thought, but without overthinking it, she flipped the pages all the way back to where she remembered leaving Tom's adventures. She landed on page 52. "Nope, I've read this already." On to page 53. "I've read this as well." She skimmed through page 54 and stopped at the third paragraph of page 55. "Here we are!"

She took a sip of hot cocoa and as she set eyes on the page again, something caught her attention. It was some sort of side note. Every so often she'd write thoughts or comments when reading a book, but she hadn't written anything down on this one yet.

Florence read it and what she read made her shudder.

This is only the beginning.

There was something eerie about that sentence. But the shudders faded away when she found a sensible explanation to what had probably happened: it was a used book, so surely the previous owner had written it down. Still, Florence found it a bit odd. "Why would anyone state such an obvious remark?" she thought. Of course it was the beginning. It was only the end of chapter four and anyone could see there were still thirty-one more to go. She decided not to judge the previous owner so harshly and carry on with her morning.

Florence considered herself a fast reader. But she also saw this as a problem. Some of the books were so good she guzzled them down. Her eyes could barely follow her wish to know what came next. She always got to the end too quickly and then there came a feeling of emptiness and the excruciating need to find the next book as soon as possible.

That's why she practised the art of what she liked to call *delicate reading*. "And how does one do that exactly?" Grandpa Davey asked her once.

"It's a very simple technique. It means reading with good manners. You could also call it ladylike reading. You just have to read slowly, very gently. You don't want to choke," Florence said. "Like with everything, at first this takes practice because you start to speed up without even knowing. You have to force yourself to slow down. As time goes by, it comes naturally. You barely have to think about it. Sometimes I read a chapter twice simply because one time isn't enough."

That morning at Grandpa Davey's, as she took another sip of cocoa, Florence decided to spend the entire day on chapters five and six. Tom Sawyer and his adventures kept her from doing other things she had to do. She wanted to visit Ignatius and Mr Caroling, and most of all, she wanted to see Hephy. But the book was like a spider's web that had trapped her and would not let go, so she figured it was not entirely her fault. Besides, she still had plenty of time to go see everybody. Her friends wouldn't mind. They were Inkwellers after all. They would understand that a book could do that to a person.

The Story of Grandpa Davey

Shaped by time and weather, Grandpa Davey's cottage was a crooked dwelling, with a humble character and the smell of warm baked bread. It was on Vellum Boulevard, right on the south edge of the town. Made of stone and timber, it had dormer windows, ancient doorways and a curious staircase where each step had a different height.

Florence came running down those steps in search of breakfast. Grandpa Davey was not only the owner of the bookshop, but he was also famous for inventing the craziest and most delicious dishes. Florence walked inside the kitchen and sat at the table. A pot of cocoa was heating up on the stove. Grandpa Davey was setting the bagel bracelets and blueberry necklaces on a platter. To go with this edible jewellery, he had prepared his Colossal Croissants. Lighter than air, the secret ingredient to their huge size remained unknown to everyone except the chef.

Grandpa Davey and Florence talked about how telephone calls crossed the oceans and how cars could turn their headlights on if they were not plugged into a wall. Though she had her own theories, she suspected Grandpa Davey's explanations were the proper ones. How did he manage to have the right answers to every question?

Grandpa Davey was indeed a splendid first-class granddad. Though a tad bewildering on occasions, he had lived the most extraordinary life, and Florence knew every detail of every anecdote. She never got tired of hearing them.

There were, of course, some bits that were her favourites, starting with the fact that he smoked a pipe, he fancied singing happy birthday when it was no one's birthday and he loved the sound of chewing and slurping. He cheered with pompoms whenever someone made a lot of noise drinking soda or eating toasted almonds.

Florence had actually made a shortlist of all her favourite Grandpa stories and she called them *Greatest Snippets of a Life Extraordinaire*.

It went as follows:

Greatest Snippet Number One

Grandpa Davey wasn't an original Inkweller. He was born far away from the town, but life and its thousand twists and turns and ups and downs eventually led him to the bookshop in Inkwell. There was one more thing that steered him to that town: the fact that he had a peculiar view of the world and a curious spirit. Grandpa Davey's destiny would have turned out quite different if he'd been a cautious, shy and hesitant person.

His philosophy in life was to walk towards the uncomfortable and step on it as though it were a doormat. He believed that of all the gloomy thoughts a person could have, doubt was the most dangerous one. So he would often fry his doubts, make French toast out of them and eat them with maple syrup.

Greatest Snippet Number Two

Grandpa Davey had been the pilot of a blimp. With it, he crossed deserts, jungles and oceans. The airship travelled slowly, but it travelled far. And since blimps fly quite low in the sky, he could often see people on the ground waving at him, and if he wasn't doing a daring manoeuvre with the rudder, he gave a wave back.

Every so often, he picked a random spot on his map, flew over there and did a serious expedition of the area. Thanks to these expeditions, he ate all kinds of food, learned over fifteen languages and travelled round the world three times.

One day, fairly tired of travelling, he resolved it was time for a change. He landed his blimp on a small town near the sea. There were only a few houses, fewer people, a grocery store, a couple of fishing boats on the shore and a lighthouse that stood at the top of a lonely ragged rock.

He got a job there, guiding boats to avoid dangerous waters. "We lighthouse keepers have to make sure boats can find their way through the night," Grandpa Davey liked to say about his new job.

With some of the money he'd saved from working at the lighthouse, he purchased a penny-farthing bike. He also bought a top hat to wear while riding it.

"Now we are talking! This is how I like to roll!" he said during his first ride on it. He felt so good sitting high up on that humungous front wheel, looking at everything that was going on around him.

On one of his rides, as he tried to pedal across the Great Grumbling Grasslands, he spotted a discombobulated man looking in every possible direction.

"Hello there, young fella!" Grandpa Davey shouted from the top of his penny-farthing.

"Oh… Hello."

"You look a bit lost."

"I am lost! See, I had found a great new idea for my new novel, but then it slipped off my hands and the wind kept taking it further and further away. I ran as fast as I could chasing it…

But I never caught it. And by the time I gave up trying, I was lost and so far away from home. I was never able to map my way back."

"You're a writer?"

"Yes. Some say I'm a hopelessly romantic writer, but I like to think I'm just a daydreamer. But that might have been what made me lose my idea, and my hometown."

"And what town would that be?"

The writer looked at the stranger before him. He seemed to hesitate for a moment, but then answered the question. "It's called Inkwell."

"Huh… I've never heard of it before."

"That's because it's sort of a hidden place. Few people know it exists."

"Like a secret town?"

"Something like that."

"Why is it hidden?"

"Protection."

"From whom?"

"It's a long story…"

"Who lives there?"

"Very special people. Mainly, Inkwell is a town of storytellers, like yours truly." The writer pointed at himself. "But there's also an Inkweller who's a nutty yet terribly talented inventor, an Inkweller that bakes every kind of chocolate treat, another who makes cuckoo clocks, and I don't know if you like trees, but we have the most beautiful maple tree in our main square."

"I do like maple trees. Please, tell me more about this town of yours."

"I would say it's an otherworldly place. And most important to me, it's…home."

"Well, if that's the case, I will help you find your way back."

"Really?"

"Yes, really."

"But you don't know where it is?"

"Don't worry, young fella, I have what we need to get us out of this pickle." Grandpa Davey searched inside his jacket pocket and pulled out a folded piece of paper. "First rule of travelling: never leave without a map. Mind you, I never actually usually use it. But when the time comes, like now, it's good to have one. Let's see. We're here, in the Great Grumbling Grasslands. Some wombats I saw earlier told me the name of this place. I came from the west, so it's safe to say Inkwell is not that way. If we go east though, and we cross the Riveting River Valley and the Wood of Whispering Weeping Willows…"

"Oh, look, at the edge of the map, can you see it? It's the letter I…a bit blurry, but it's there."

"Do you think that's some sort of code for Inkwell?" Grandpa Davey asked.

"It must be. I do remember going through this awful wood full of creepy weeping willows."

"Then it must be it. There's only one way to find out. Let's go." Grandpa Davey got on his bike. "By the way, what's your name?"

"Jakob."

"Jakob, I'm Davey. Climb aboard!"

With a turn of a little knob on the handlebar of the penny-farthing, a second seat popped up and Jakob hopped onto it. They rode along freely through the Great Grumbling Grassland, merrily through the Riveting River Valley and really quickly through the Wood of Whispering Weeping Willows.

Greatest Snippet Number Three

When they arrived in Inkwell, Jakob hopped off the penny-farthing and walked to the main square. Grandpa Davey followed him on the bike. When they got to the maple tree, Jakob looked up. Its golden leaves greeted him with the softest flutter.

It was Mr McGlue, the bookbinder, who happened to be walking across the main square, that saw him first.

"Jakob?" he asked. "Is that you?"

"It's me, Mr McGlue, I'm back!"

All Inkwellers stopped what they were doing and came running to the square. Jakob must have got over a dozen hugs, for Inkwellers loved to hug. They considered it a wholesome habit that could cure or mend almost anything.

When the big fuzz dwindled, Grandpa Davey was about to hop again on his penny-farthing but Mr Caroling, the town's calligrapher, stopped him.

"You can't leave just now, Mr Davey!" the calligrapher said. "You must stay the night. You are now a great hero here in Inkwell, a premium citizen if you will, and following our tradition, we will throw a party in your honour. Please, be so kind as to accept our invitation."

"Then I'd be delighted to stay," Grandpa Davey said.

~

At one point during the party, a girl with big hazel eyes, sleek brown ringlets and the right combination of elegance and cheekiness walked towards Grandpa Davey and with the simplest of manners said what she wanted to say. For Grandpa Davey, it was love at first word.

"Thank you for helping Jakob."

"It was my pleasure."

"Where do you hail from?"

"I'm a traveller, I hail from all over the world."

"A dauntless adventurer. It's nice to meet you…"

"Davey… My name is Davey."

"Davey, I'm Winifred."

"What about you, Winifred?"

"I've never travelled anywhere. I've lived here all my life."

"Well, this town of yours, it seems pretty special."

"Comely, becoming and flamboyant, that's how Inkwell always was and how it will always be."

Grandpa Davey looked at the starry sky and then at Winifred. Although the party went on with the racket of music playing and people dancing, for Grandpa Davey time slowed down as he wished he could listen to her forever.

"Soon you'll come to see, should you decide to stay here," Winifred said, "Inkwell is no dalliance, it will become your eternal love, your place of belonging."

"I think it already has," Grandpa Davey said, and he knew then he would never leave that town. He had found his final destination.

Greatest Snippet Number Four

One morning, ambling around the narrow streets of Inkwell, Grandpa Davey walked by a quaint old bookshop. He walked inside and as soon as the bell in the entrance door tinkled, he knew that was the place where he wanted to work.

"Do you, by any chance, happen to have any job openings?" Grandpa Davey asked.

"Do you know anything about books?" the man behind the counter said.

"Well, I used to work in a lighthouse. It was quite a solitary job and the previous keepers had left many books behind. There's a tight bond between loneliness and reading, you know. I guess those books were my only friends while I was there."

71

"I haven't had an assistant in years…but then again, that was the kind of answer I like. Can you start tomorrow?"

"Of course."

"Good. My name is Mr Quill and I'm the owner of this bookshop."

Grandpa Davey began his work there at once. Of all the jobs he'd had in his life, this was the one that suited him best.

Mr Quill was a thin man, with a heart-shaped face and funny dishevelled hair. He kept running his hands through it, trying to make it neat, but it just rebelled and sprang up, making him look like a porcupine. His voice had a soothing tone and he never fumbled for words because he always knew what to say.

One afternoon in the bookshop, while they were mending the spines of the oldest books, Grandpa Davey asked Mr Quill, "What is the greatest word in the world?"

"Well, that depends. It will be different for every person."

"You mean there are no rules?"

"There are a few rules. But you have to remember that a word can be great because of its meaning, like *sublime* or *blessing* or *agreement*. Or it can be beautiful because of the way it sounds, like *labyrinthine* or *cerulean* or *whimsy*…"

"Or *cinder*, *caprice* and *gale*."

"But I believe it always comes down to personal taste and the experience we've had with each word."

"And which is your favourite word?"

"I have to admit, I have a crush on the words that have the letter b and the letter l in them, like *blob* or *bubble* or *quibble* or *pebble*. What about you?"

"*Winifred*."

"Ah, you see, that's a name, and the thing with names is that when pronounced they automatically take us to the person we know has that name. It's like a reflex."

"So we can't escape it?"

"Nope, we can't. Names remind us of specific people, so they can be the greatest words or the most horrendous ones. They can even make you feel sick and turn your stomach upside down, like for example... *Jeffrey*, which anyone might argue is quite a lovely name, but to me, ewww! It reminds me of this boy I once met who never washed his hair, had dirt underneath his fingernails and he always had tomato sauce stains all over his clothes."

"Interesting theory," Grandpa Davey said, "but then I'm not sure yet which is my favourite word. I guess I'll have to find it."

"You will, probably when you least expect it. It might even be one of those words that are beautiful both because of the way it sounds and its meaning, like... *bagel*. It sounds plump and fluffy and when you say it you can't help but think of one of those yummy bread rolls and your mouth starts watering."

"What happens with the contrary? Words that have a hideous meaning, like *abominable* or *snot* or *leech*?"

"Simple. You get the opposite effect. If you say *rotten* or *fester*, you'll all of a sudden be surrounded by a bitter maggoty smell. Or, in my case, the word that always does the trick is *tired*. If I think *tired*, I start yawning right away. The words we use shape our world. They are the bricks with which we build our days. So if you have a choice, why choose saying an ugly word that will make you feel unhappy? It's always better to go for good words. It simply makes sense."

Greatest Snippet Number Five

At the old bookshop, Grandpa Davey stumbled upon his fondness for books and discovered the truest love one can have for the written word. Mr Quill taught him everything he knew: how to explore a library and find its hidden treasures, how to sip stories one sentence at a time and how to tell the difference between the good books and the not so good ones.

While working in the bookshop, Grandpa Davey built the cosy crooked cottage with the dormer windows and the uneven staircase for him and Winifred. In the afternoons, Grandpa Davey cooked rainbow whoopie pies while Winifred knitted fluffy sweater vests and very long scarves, and every evening before dinner the couple danced with agile steps to the tunes of a gramophone. Years went by with this never-boring routine.

But few things last forever.

One day, when the seasons were changing and the dry winds of the north had begun to blow, Grandpa Davey walked into the bookshop to find Mr Quill with his hat on and a suitcase next to him.

"Are you going somewhere?" Grandpa Davey asked.

"I'm going on a long-awaited journey."

"How nice, holidays."

"This isn't really a holiday."

"Oh… Will you be coming back soon?"

"No, this is a long journey."

"But we have the Fantasy Book Fair next month."

"I'm sorry, Davey, this has been a sort of last-minute invitation, and it's an invitation I've been waiting for quite a while."

"Will you come back at all?"

"Who knows, maybe one day. But that's a promise I cannot make today. For now, this is a one-way ticket journey."

"Where are you going?"

"The thing is…that's something I cannot tell you. At least not yet."

"Is it far?"

"All I can tell you is that I'm going beyond the Mountains of the East."

"That does sound far away."

"It is. That's why I wanted to tell you something."

"Anything."

"My bookshop is now yours, if you'll have it."

"Really?"

"Really. There's no one better suited for the job. Will you take good care of it?"

"Of course I will. But…"

"Yes, Davey, what is it?"

"Well, it's just that… I'm gonna miss you, Mr Quill. I wish we had more time together."

"I'd like that too, very much. But nothing is as sorrowful as it seems. Life is simple and it's never unfair. Remember that."

"I promise I will."

"Oh… One more thing. I almost forgot. Here."

Mr Quill handed Grandpa Davey a rough-hewn key.

"But I already have keys for the bookshop."

"This doesn't open the bookshop."

"What does it open?"

"The old cabinet."

"The one in the hidden corner past the mystery books and adventure novels?"

"Yes, that one."

"But that's the one that has the…"

"It is."

"But I don't know how to…"

"You will when the time comes."

Last but not least, Greatest Snippet Number Six:
The tale of how she came to be…

Life kept rolling on.

Grandpa Davey and Grandma Winifred had a daughter, Lexi. In time, Lexi grew up to be independent, scary smart and a lover of numbers and everything they had to offer.

Things with numbers, thought Lexi, were clean, simple and logical. There was no *maybe* to be found in them. No place for misinterpretations. Numbers were natural, whole and real. Although, she hated to admit, sometimes they could turn out to be negative, irrational and complex. But even so, Lexi couldn't help but love the curvy shape of the 8 and the 3, the sharp lines of the 1 and the 7, the opposite beauty of the 9 and the 6 and the unbroken style of the 0.

The day she turned eighteen, Lexi made the unexpected decision to leave Inkwell and move to the city to study this matter of numbers in greater depth at the Odd School, a peculiar college where gifted students dived head first into the eccentric (in some cases) and even (in many others) universe of mathematics.

It was the day after she set foot in the Odd School that she fell in love with Mr Percy Ibbot, a brilliant mathematician with a healthy craving for solving equations and finding the best solutions to problems. By a simple symmetric property, Mr Percy Ibbot fell in love with Lexi. Together they had a daughter who they named Florence.

The Attack

A week went by at Grandpa Davey's cottage. The night chased the day seven times, without being able to catch it. Snow kept falling over the streets and rooftops of Inkwell, keeping them white and icy. Florence read her book every morning and afternoon, partaking in the adventures of Tom Sawyer and his friend Huck. Grandpa Davey went to the bookshop every day and Florence dropped in at noon to have lunch together in a little sandwich place on the corner of Calligram Street and Pulp Lane. Soon, an unlit sky and its shy new moon were round the corner.

It was almost nightfall when Florence walked into the kitchen to find Grandpa Davey looking into the pantry.

"What's for tonight's menu?" she asked.

"I think I'm going to make some marmalade ravioli," he answered.

"Didn't we have that yesterday for lunch and dinner?" Florence said, laughing.

Grandpa Davey nodded, a cheeky grin on his face. Of all the mouth-watering dishes he'd invented, his favourite was the marmalade ravioli. Although he knew one should stop eating even before feeling full, he could eat three helpings in a row as if he were a bottomless piggy bank. He was also a fan of porridge for supper. There was something amusing about eating at night something that's supposed to be eaten early in the morning.

"Fine, you're right, you're right. I'll surprise you with something different this evening," he said as he grabbed a few things from the pantry.

"Excellent! Give me a shout when it's ready. I'll be upstairs reading."

She ran to her room, grabbed her book, opened it where the bookmark was and placed him on the desk. Then she leaned back on a rocking armchair that was near the window and began to read.

৯

Ben lay quietly on the desk, looking at Florence while she read. He kept completely silent, though deep down he really wanted to say a lot. "Should I tell her I'm alive?" he thought. "No…or maybe yes. Or no, not yet, maybe later… On second thoughts, it should be now. Yes, now! Oh, but look at her, she's really into her book, I can't do it right now. I'll do it later, tomorrow perhaps." He sighed and continued his inner talk. "Why am I so nervous, I've been doing a great job, haven't I?"

৯

Florence sat at the dining table with Grandpa Davey. The menu that evening: spongy star-shaped pancakes with sprinkled cheese and smashed eggs, dipped peanut butter logs, and fruit pizza for dessert. They enjoyed every bite until they felt like two big birthday balloons ready to pop.

"That fruit pizza, I think it was your best yet," Florence said.

"I know it's your favourite. It was your Grandma's favourite too."

"Was it? I didn't know that."

"That and my rainbow whoopie pies."

"Do you miss her, Grandpa?"

"Always. Every day."

78

"I can't imagine what it must be like, missing someone every day."

"At first it was the hardest thing. When she was gone, I grasped that all too soon the day comes when there are no more days left. I was heartbroken and there was nothing but ache in my heart."

"How did you get past that?"

"It wasn't easy, and it took me a long time. But one day I decided it was time to try something."

"Something like what?"

"You see, your Grandma was the happiest person I'd ever known. I figured I couldn't let sorrow overwhelm me. She wouldn't want that. So I would take a minute to hug her in my imagination and that, curiously, led the sad feeling away, if only a little. As time went by, only the good memories remained. Now every time I see something that belongs to her, I don't feel sad. Like when I see her thimble collection, for example."

"The one that's on the shelf above the dining room table?"

"That very one. She used to embroider handkerchiefs for everyone in Inkwell. People wanted to catch a cold just so she would make a hankie for them."

"Tell me more about her."

"What would you like to know?"

"Her favourite thing to knit?"

"Really long scarves."

"And her favourite book character?"

"It was a tie."

"Between?"

"Gulliver, Sherlock Holmes and the Mad Hatter."

∞

Later on, they went into the living room and sat by the fireplace.

Grandpa Davey plopped himself into a brown armchair and Florence tossed a furry cushion on the floor and sat down, placing one leg across the other. Grandpa Davey cleared his throat, getting ready for one of his after-supper tales.

"Which story is it tonight?" Florence asked eagerly. "Is it the one where you drove the ice cream van?"

Grandpa Davey had indeed once owned an ice cream van and through the large sliding window that acted as a serving hatch, he sold the weirdest flavours of ice cream he had, of course, thoughtfully invented. There was candied corn, garlicky tangerine, salmon and cinnamon, prickle-free cactus, and sticky salty sweet potato. To everyone's surprise, he became an utter sensation with kids, a handful of courageous adults, and some tail-wagging pets.

The truck's distinctive melodic chime was expected in every town and village. Children ran out into the road at the sight of the pink little truck and on more than one occasion Grandpa Davey got startled when kids appeared without warning like a herd of elephants with empty stomachs.

"No, it's not the ice cream story," Grandpa Davey said. "Tonight I'm going to tell you a tale about the history of Inkwell."

The room was completely silent except for the soft crackling of the fire.

"I don't think you've ever told me a story about Inkwell's history before."

"I haven't, but I think today is a fine day to tell you this story."

"OK then, by all means, please begin."

"Very well, here we go… A long *looong* time ago, this village was the cradle of the most legendary writers and storytellers."

"But I thought Inkwell still was the home of great writers and storytellers?"

"True, it still is, but back then it was different."

"What do you mean?"

"Do you know where the town took its name from?"

"I don't actually."

"You know the water well in the main square?"

"Yes."

"No one really knows who built it, or when…and what's even stranger, it never provided water."

"What was down there then?"

"Allerian Ink," Grandpa Davey said, and after a short pause added, "Also known as the Ink of a Thousand Beginnings."

"What's Allerian Ink? Why was it called Ink of a Thousand Beginnings? What did it do? Was it magical? What colour was it?" Dozens of questions piled up in Florence's mouth, but these were the ones that managed to get out first.

"How do stories begin?" Grandpa Davey answered. "How do you choose the first sentence of a book? How do you pick the first word for a story? Well, Allerian Ink was an unending source of magical beginnings. Every drop of Allerian Ink had the seed for a story to be born." Florence listened to Grandpa Davey without making a sound. "The writers would draw up Allerian Ink with buckets and when they dipped their quills in it, the greatest ideas were inspired. And so it happened that Inkwell became the village of the guardians of words. They all pledged to defend them, knowing the power they had."

"Few people understand that, right, Grandpa, that words have power?"

"Very few, unfortunately, but as precious a gift words are, we must be very careful with them."

"What do you mean by that exactly?" Florence asked, placing the palms of her hands near the fire to warm up.

"We don't want to utter what we'll later regret. The words that come out of our mouths go into the world and echo forever."

"But the well is now dry. What happened?"

"It's a mystery. No one knows how or why the well dried up…or no one really remembers. All that remained was the name, Inkwell," Grandpa Davey said.

"I wonder what went on. What could possibly have happened in this town?"

"I've asked myself that question hundreds of times."

"I guess the old maple tree in the main square is the only witness who remembers."

"That may very well be the case."

"How do you know all this?"

"Mr Quill told me this story many years ago."

"And how does the story continue?"

"Oh, right, right." Grandpa Davey resumed his storytelling. "Not only writers and linguists lived in Inkwell…"

"Grandpa," Florence interrupted, tucking her hair behind her ear, "is a linguist someone who is an expert on language?"

"On the mark, my dear. A linguist is someone who is an expert on language. They study the way language works and they tend to be skilled in foreign languages as well."

"A linguist studies the way language works and is usually skilled in foreign languages as well," Florence repeated and then memorized, catalogued and filed the new piece of knowledge for future use.

"So, as I was saying, not only writers and linguists lived here, but also bookbinders, papermakers, calligraphers, illustrators and librarians, all committed to being the best guardians of the written word. As time went by, other craftspeople and artisans made their way to Inkwell, and though it was a small village, it never refused entrance to anyone. Hence, Inkwell welcomed an inventor, a chocolatier, a blacksmith, a clockmaker and many other new residents…" Before Grandpa Davey got to the end, Florence yawned three times in a row. "Well, I think it's time to go to bed. I'll finish the story some other day," Grandpa Davey said as Florence made a huge effort to wake up just a tiny bit for the annoying minutes of teeth brushing.

Outside it was snowing. Pearly flakes glided down through the air before landing smoothly on the ground. Inkwell was swiftly covered with white silence. A new moon was hidden in the sky. Grandpa Davey walked his granddaughter to her bedroom and tucked her in. Since it was a cold winter night, he took one of Grandma Winifred's hand-knitted blankets out of the wardrobe and placed it on top of the bed. He turned off the lights and shortly after, comfy sleep cap on, he was also asleep and snoring.

∞

Inside *The Adventures of Tom Sawyer*, Ben had also fallen asleep. Most of the words in the book were also sleeping. A few were still awake.

"Are you up, *Restless*?" *Alert* asked.

"Of course," *Restless* replied.

"What time is it anyway?"

"No idea."

And then *Exact* whispered, "It will be midnight in four, three, two…"

When *Exact* said *one*, she saw that Ben's body started to shake. At first it was a soft jiggle but soon it became a seriously rough trembling.

Alert tried to wake Ben up but the bookmark was

84

fast asleep. Helpless, the words saw how Ben was swiftly transformed. The mushroom-like ears popped up once again on the top of his head. The row of spikes sprung on his back and the leathery, thick tail on his bottom. The words could smell the hideous Brussels sprout odour coming out of Pox's greenish black skin.

"Well hello there, little words, did you miss me?" Pox said.

The words didn't utter a word. Although instead of being petrified with fear like last time, they were paying close attention to what Pox was saying. There was something in the imp's voice. It had a dash of sorcery.

"How about we play hide and seek?" Pox suggested with the draw of a snake charmer. "Would you like that? It's such a fun game, don't you think? And I bet I can find you all!"

The imp closed his eyes and counted to thirteen. While he did this, all the words in the book ran as fast as they could. They got mixed up, they climbed, they slid to the edges of the pages, they swapped places so as not to be found by the imp.

❧

When the sun rose, Pox the imp was gone and Ben the bookmark was back. The tail had vanished. So had the spikes. The mushroom-like ears had shrunk and the big pleated cap was again on the bookmark's head. The crispy air of dawn had brought back Ben's kind, droopy eyes.

❧

Like every morning, Florence sat at her desk with her cup of cocoa, this time with six marshmallows in it. She opened *The Adventures of Tom Sawyer* but as soon as she set eyes on the page, she saw that nothing made sense.

She couldn't read anything. She flipped page after page. It was all a complete mess. Most of the sentences were gone because the words were piled up on the edges of the pages or wedged on the binder of the book.

The sentences that were still there were ruled by complete disorder. Dialogues were nothing but absurd. There were commas beside stops, crammed verbs and adjectives that did not chaperone anybody. There was a "*He*" followed by a "*them*" and a "*one*" that "*noise under black, boy yet while around garments: away!*" There was no logic left. The book's meaning had hidden with the words. The story was gone.

Discoveries

Florence ran out of her room, rushed down the stairs and stormed into the living room. Grandpa Davey was sitting in his brown armchair lighting up his pipe and blowing big puffs of smoke that smelled like wood and dark chocolate.

"Grandpa! Grandpa!"

"What is it?"

"My book! Look at this!"

"What happened?"

"It's the words! They're out of their place!"

"Calm down, my dear!" Grandpa Davey said in a husky yet soothing voice. "What do you mean 'out of their place'? Let me have a look."

He hooked the bookmark with his finger, opened the book, drew on his pipe and pondered. Florence looked at him, expecting an answer straight away, but Grandpa Davey didn't say anything. He was in a deeply concentrated thinking mode, making acknowledging sounds like "*Hmmm*" and "*Hum*" and "*Hem*" as he turned the pages. When he got to the end, he closed the book and placed it on the coffee table, then he put the bookmark on top of it. With a little bit of effort, Grandpa Davey stood up.

"How did this happen?" he asked.

"I have no idea," Florence answered.

"This is serious." He looked at his granddaughter. "We have to go, my dear."

"Where are we going?" Florence asked.

"To the bookshop," Grandpa Davey answered. "I think I may know where we can find a clue to what has happened here. There's a very old book that…"

"It's not my fault, I swear!" Ben said suddenly. "I don't know what happened. I went to sleep last night and woke up amid all this mighty awful turmoil! I don't remember anything! Oh, what have I done?"

Grandpa Davey's eyebrows quirked and stayed quirked, and a thunderbolt of shock swept over Florence. She stared at the little bookmark in front of her. For the first time since she could remember, she could not find a word to utter.

"I said I was sorry! Very sorry… Hello? Are you OK there?" Ben said, jumping off the book and onto the coffee table. "I've been meaning to introduce myself before but I never seemed to find the right time. I am deeply apologetic."

"What's going on here?"

"I'm your bookmark. Ben!"

"Is this possible?" Florence asked.

"Of course it's possible," Ben answered. "You made me. Because you are a very inventive girl, you created a very original bookmark: me."

"But… I don't underst… I mean… How can…?" Florence stammered, looking at Ben and then at Grandpa Davey, and then at Ben, and then at Grandpa Davey again, as if she were watching a ping-pong match. "But… How?"

"The two lines of the poem you sang," Ben answered.

"Blake's poem?" Florence asked.

"Aha," Ben said.

"*Every morn and every night, some are born to sweet delight.*" Florence said as she remembered singing those lines the morning she made Ben.

"Oh my! oh my! oh my!" Grandpa Davey said. "This is… I don't know what this is. This is extraordinary, Florence. Oh my! Look at what you've created!"

"But you're alive!" Florence said, looking at Ben.

"Indeed I am. Very much so."

"But I can't believe it," Florence said.

"But you should believe it," Ben said.

"But I can't!" Florence said.

"Why not?" Ben asked.

"I… I don't really know why," Florence said. "I just feel it's unbelievable."

"But I'm here. I'm Ben. I'm talking to you. You made me with your words."

"I did?" Florence asked.

"All I can say is, my dear," Grandpa Davey said, "I've been round the world long enough to know that sometimes impossible things become possible. Anyone is capable of things beyond the bounds of possibility."

"Huh…" Florence had to mull over everything for a few seconds. The brainy girl that she was, she had to process all this information. She could feel her brain running at maximum power, like popcorn in a pressure cooker. She had created a kite that could point the way to where she wanted to go, a cake that made people laugh, a beanie that took away bad dreams and a folding fan that made her hair smell like jasmine when she swished it, so why wouldn't she be able to make a savvy book-mark that could talk and think and jump? Her conclusion then: indeed, she believed in things beyond the bounds of possibility. She got down on her knees, so as to be at the same height as Ben, who was still standing on the coffee table. She extended her hand in greeting. Ben smiled back and shook her hand.

"Very well then, it's nice to meet you, Ben."

"Oh, it's my pleasure!" And he did a gentle bow.

"I think I'll just go make myself a cup of tea so you two can chat for a while, get to know each other," Grandpa Davey said as he grabbed his pipe and walked to the kitchen.

In the living room, Florence had sat on the floor and Ben on the edge of the coffee table. There was a short, slightly awkward silence, those that come when two people don't really know how to begin a conversation. It was Ben who threw the awkward silence aside.

"I'm over the moon I can finally talk to you." He wanted to yell it with his arms wide open; instead, he chose to say it in a mannerly voice, but then he tossed all decorum aside and his words gushed out of his mouth like water out of a firefighter's hose. "I'm so over the moon I am finally talking to you! I wish I'd been braver and had the courage to talk to you sooner, but oh well, it is what it is. There is no point in regretting the things we did or did not do. No point at all. The true point is I'm over the moon! I'm thrilled! Thrilled, I'll tell you! I wish to be your good friend! And I wish to be your best bookmark! And there are other things that I wish, but I can tell you about them later. We have all the time in the world…" Ben stopped talking abruptly and looked at Florence. "Then again…"

"What is it?" Florence asked.

"I'm not sure if we have all the time in the world."

"Why do you say that?"

"I think something happened to me last night. I don't remember much. It's all very fuzzy. I do know it felt horrible. Something monstrous, Florence, and whatever it was, I had no power to fight it."

"It must be related to what happened with the words in the book."

"I'm so sorry, Florence, I was born to be your bookmark

and I've failed. I've failed you. And I've failed the words. It's revolting! What a disgrace!" Tears began to well in Ben's eyes.

"Don't cry, Ben, it's not your fault." She was now holding him in the palm of her hand.

"It's just that, sometimes at night," Ben said, sobbing, "I would talk to the words. I tried to teach them how meaningful they are and that without them human beings would simply be too lost, and then... KAPSHHH!" He did an exploding gesture with his hands. "Everything was ruined, smashed up by whatever I became."

"Do you remember anything else?" Florence said.

"Oh, I don't know. It felt...as if something took over me and I couldn't do anything, I couldn't move or speak or anything!"

"Did you, by any chance, feel the same thing last week? Before you appeared in a different page?"

"It's all such a blur," Ben said as he tried to recall.

"We must find out what happened," she said.

Grandpa Davey came into the living room with his cup of tea. He sat down in his armchair, took a sip and looked at Ben.

"Hi there," Ben said, looking back at him.

"Hello," Grandpa Davey said, examining the little bookmark. He took another sip of the tea and turned his gaze to Florence. "Oh my, oh my, I can't help but wonder how you do all these things, my dear?" Grandpa Davey said.

"I've never given much thought to it actually," Florence said. "But then something Ben said to me got me thinking."

"What's that?" Grandpa Davey asked.

"The two lines from the poem I sang."

"Aha." Grandpa Davey nodded. "One of your favourites."

"Exactly," Florence said. "Well, the day I made the

91

folding fan, I sang another favourite poem of mine: '*Houses and rooms are full of perfumes…the shelves are crowded with perfumes, I breathe the fragrance myself, and know it and like it.*'"

"Walt Whitman," Grandpa Davey said.

"And when I was making the beanie hat that takes away bad dreams, it was Kipling's poetry I kept repeating: '*If you can dream, and not make dreams your master, if you can think, and not make thoughts your aim; If you can meet with Triumph and Disaster and treat those two impostors just the same.*'"

"What about the kite that points to where you want to go and the velvety vanilla cake that makes you laugh madly?" Grandpa Davey was seriously intrigued.

"Let me think," Florence said. "I believe it was an old poem about travelling and a quirky ode to laughter."

"So it's your way with words," Grandpa Davey said.

"Right, words…" Florence looked at the book on the coffee table. "Grandpa, we have to do something about this."

"Yes, we have to," Grandpa Davey said.

"What do you think we are up against?" she asked.

"To be honest, my darling, I'm not sure, and I'd rather not speak of uncertain things. But we should get to the bookshop at once."

The Day Stories Disappeared

It was a quiet morning in Inkwell. Florence, Ben and Grandpa Davey left the cottage and walked down Vellum Boulevard. Then they took Italics Lane, a peculiar street where all the houses were tilted just a few inches to the right, making the passers-by feel askew. Ben travelled in Grandpa Davey's tweed jacket pocket. He popped his head out and peeped around.

"What's that smell?" Ben asked.

"It's the smell of wintry morning air," Grandpa Davey told him.

"And what's that?" Ben asked, pointing forward.

"A drinking fountain," Florence said, "covered in untouched snow."

"Snow… It's so white. And what about that?"

"What? This wooden-pole fence?" Grandpa Davey asked.

"No, that sound," Ben answered.

"That's a woodpecker. See, over there, hammering that tree trunk," Grandpa Davey said.

"Everything is so real in real life," Ben said.

As they were approaching the main square, they heard a commotion. When they turned the corner of Colloquy Street, they saw a crowd under the old maple tree arguing and using one too many despicable gestures. More people kept coming out from their houses, most of them yelling.

"The library!" Lorelai, the librarian, cried. "All the words in the books have gone crazy! They're anywhere but where they ought to be!"

"Same thing happened in the book I'm reading! All the words are jumbled up, and some aren't even in the book! They're just gone!" another confused Inkweller yelled.

"I tried to make a chocolate cake today and a sticky lump came out. My recipes are all scrambled! *Mon Dieu, quelle pagaille!*" Monsieur Pépite, the chocolatier, grieved as he showed everybody the disaster of a cake he'd baked.

"And my translations, look at this! All the languages are entwined!" said Trevor, the translator, the one in charge of making sure that things written in English were understood by people who spoke other languages, and that stories in other languages were understood by those who spoke only English.

"What has happened in our town?" Mr McGlue, the bookbinder, demanded of no one in particular.

"How can I illustrate what I cannot read?" Imogen, the illustrator, snivelled.

"My manuscripts!" wailed Percival, the poised poet, who at this point had lost all his grace. "The rhyme is gone from every line of my poems."

As Florence, Grandpa Davey and Ben walked past the newsstand near the square, Florence caught a glimpse of the main headline of the *Inkwell Herald*.

BREAKING NEWS!

THE DAY STORIES DISAPPEARED IN THE WORLD

"Grandpa, wait!" Florence said as she gave a coin to the newsboy and grabbed the copy that was on top of the pile of newspapers. "Hear this," she said as she began to read the article.

In every library of every city, in every book on every bedside table, words have gone crazy and are anywhere but where they ought to be. The world has never seen such a thing. Authorities are still working to make sense out of this and try to apprehend the culprit of this awful crime.

Experts on the matter say that the consequences of last night's events are catastrophic. Much that once was written is now unwritten and there is no one to bring those stories back and recount them to others.

Love letters have become messages impossible to decipher and many hearts have been reported broken. Peace treaties are being decoded as war declarations. The Post Office cannot do its job since no address matches the proper resident.

Bus drivers, aviators and train conductors can't get to their destinations because the names of neighbourhoods and kingdoms have swapped locations in every map. This has also caused problems for all the sailors who were led astray in the vast loneliness of the seas with no guide from the now useless cartograms, charts and atlases.

Musical notes have concealed themselves behind pentagrams. Witnesses at the Philharmonic said that musicians were only able to play screeching sounds and tuneless songs instead of symphonies, sonatas and serenades.

Laws, decrees and constitutions have disappeared since all the words that made them have been camouflaged beneath one another. Without rules to ensure order, trouble rose and spread contagiously in several towns and villages.

To make matters worse, verbs have disguised as adverbs. No one is able to *jump*, *think*, *eat* or *agree*. And too many *sloppily*, *rather*, *there* and *then* have been left running free. Nouns have ducked under pronouns: a *dime* under *mine*, *glee* under *she*, a *bottle of glue* went under *who*, five little *geese* dived under *these*, and a sly *spy* squatted down under *my*. Interjections have decided to lay low, losing their will to cry out and surprise with a *Hey!* or an *Oh!*

In the main square, everyone kept interrupting each other, worried about their own stories, until Florence climbed up the maple tree.

"Listen, everybody!" Her voice rang out over all the chattering. "We have to remain calm. We are Inkwellers. We cannot behave like this. We won't solve anything if we keep shouting and talking over one another. We have to be strong, and to be strong we need to stay together."

The grumble died down and everyone listened to what Florence was saying. Lorelai and Percival nodded in agreement.

Mr McGlue said, "She's right! We must stick together come what may!"

And Monsieur Pépite shouted, "*C'est tout à fait ça!*"

"We are on our way to the bookshop now where we hope to find a hint to know who's to blame for all of this," Florence said. "The words will find the way back to their place." She wasn't sure about the last sentence, but she took a chance and said it anyway.

⁂

Grandpa Davey opened the door to his old bookshop. The bell tinkled as it always did but Florence didn't run to the shelves to find a new book. This time there was little to be happy about, and there was nothing but one task ahead.

An overwhelming sadness clutched Grandpa Davey's heart when he opened some of the books and found that all the words were out of their place.

"What has happened here? All my books…"

"I'm so sorry, Grandpa," Florence said as she ran her hands over her most cherished books and then kept walking.

Grandpa Davey lit an oil lamp and went to the end of the shop. Florence and Ben followed in silence. In a hidden corner past the mystery books and adventure novels, there was an old cabinet. Grandpa Davey grabbed a rough-hewn key from his pocket.

"Many years ago," he said, "Mr Quill gave me this key…

I've never dared use it." He pushed it into the tarnished lock and opened the cabinet.

Inside, a big old book rested. It was leather-bound and had a gilt spine. The front and rear boards had bumped corners and the tail of the spine was softened and frayed. Grandpa Davey grabbed it and the wooden floor squeaked as the three of them sat down.

"Remember the other day I started telling you about the history of Inkwell?" Grandpa Davey asked, and as Florence nodded, he said, "This book is called *Lacuna Lares*. Mr Quill told me never to read it until the right moment came… Well, I think that moment has arrived."

Grandpa Davey set the book on the floor. He placed his palm on the cover and said, "*Lacuna Lares* is not so much a book but a dwelling for all the forsaken and forgotten legends. It has old knowledge, the answer to many questions, but one must know how to read it."

"Do you know how to do that, Grandpa?" Florence asked.

"No, my dear, I've never opened this book before."

"What happens if we can't read it?" Ben asked.

No one answered.

Grandpa Davey flipped the cover over. Although the pages were thick, they also seemed to be brittle, as if they would crack if one turned them over too fast. Grandpa Davey leafed unhurriedly through them.

"But there's nothing in there," Florence whispered as she realized the pages were blank.

"I don't understand," Grandpa Davey said, scratching his forehead.

The three of them looked at each other and then looked down to the blank pages. Grandpa Davey kept flipping them slowly. Ben wore a downcast gaze, and Grandpa Davey kept scratching his forehead and drying his sweaty palms with his handkerchief. But a twinkle appeared in Florence's eyes. She didn't say anything, and even if she'd wanted to, she wouldn't have been able to explain what she felt. It was as if the book was somehow familiar to her. All of a sudden her heart was beating faster and faster and she suddenly knew what was going to happen.

Then the three of them saw it.

Words began appearing right in front of their eyes as if written by an invisible pen. The blank pages of *Lacuna Lares* were being filled with sentences in thorny handwriting. Ben was simply ossified as a fossil. Open-mouthed, he stared at the paragraphs that were cropping up all of a sudden. A story was being revealed one word at a time.

When the last word was written, Grandpa Davey sighed with relief. "This must be what we are looking for. Hopefully this will shed some light on our problem."

He read out loud the title of the story that had just sprung before them: *The Tale of the Dawn of Inkwell*.

Alodie and Zyler

The bookshop was only lit by the warm orangey flame of the oil lamp. It flickered and danced, making less threatening the silence that hovered around the place. There was a low moaning sound, perhaps nothing more than the wind blowing down the noiseless road outside the bookshop.

Inside, in the hidden corner past the mystery books and adventure novels, dust floated in the air and it made Grandpa Davey cough. He waved his hand in front of his face to ward it off. Florence and Ben were sitting on the floor with their legs crossed. Their elbows were on their knees and their chins rested on their hands.

Grandpa Davey rolled up his sleeves. He then took out his reading glasses, cleaned them with his hankie and put them on. All set, he began to read from *Lacuna Lares*. His voice came out a bit scratchy, so he cleared his throat and resumed from the beginning once again.

The Tale of the Dawn of Inkwell

There once was a time when the world was inhabited not only by men and women but by genies as well. Kind, wise and magical creatures, these genies were on Earth to help human beings become the best they could ever be.

One of these genies was called Alodie. She was a knowledge genie. Her mission was to watch over human language and protect every word that existed.

She was stunningly beautiful as well as decidedly just. She had blue hair that almost reached her feet and she wore a sculpted indigo dress. She had tender and insightful eyes and two scintillating antennae with the letter A floating on top.

Honour-bound to protect the gift of language, Alodie had the power to stir imagination in anyone who needed it with just a wiggle of her antennae. Round the world she went, helping everyone use words in the best possible way. She was known as the Word-Keeper and travelled through the skies on a little white owl named Abelard.

Sometimes she would make herself visible and sometimes she remained unseen. But one knew Alodie had been around because she always left an enchanted dandelion. If the person blew upon it, the seeds that flew away carried inspiration within them that was passed along to whomever the seeds landed on.

Alodie had an adversary. Her name was Zyler. She was a sorceress whose sole purpose was to spread ignorance and see language wither until there was nothing left of it.

Zyler was also as beautiful as Alodie, but it was a meaner beauty. She had intimidating dark eyes and swept-back red hair in a ponytail. Her sorceress' attire: a long black cape, a warrior helmet and the most ruthless demeanour. She travelled around on a cormorant that went by the name of Clemens. He had battle scars on his wings and was black as coal in a pit at night-time.

Zyler's breath had the power to wipe off the words of an entire book and with a swish of her cape, words and ideas vanished, people became suddenly blank-minded. She was known as the Word-Destroyer.

A task was one day appointed to Alodie: to build the Well of Allerian Ink in a faraway meadow in the foothills of Scriptoria Hill. That is how, past the Farm Fields of Fleeting Feathers, the Pathway of Pedantic Plum Trees, the Great Grumbling Grassland, the Riveting River Valley and the Wood of Whispering Weeping Willows, Inkwell was born.

This hidden meadow was chosen for a reason. Zyler had a special skill to smell Allerian Ink. The well needed to be safeguarded from the sorceress. But as history will show, nothing remains hidden forever. Especially when someone wants to find it.

Zyler traced the oily scent all the way through the fields, valleys and woods. She travelled at great speed on Clemens. It was not an easy hunt. Every so often, the whiff of flowers and animals made her take another route and drew her away from the Well of Allerian Ink.

Yet the day arrived.

The morning that Zyler found Inkwell, the air was icy cold and the sky was hidden above heavy grey clouds. It was dawn, but the sun was nowhere to be seen. Zyler jumped off Clemens and set foot on the main square. She walked towards the well. It only took a swish of her cape and a blow of her breath. Without warning, the Well of Allerian Ink had become forever dry.

With another swish of her cape, the wrathful sorceress brought gusts of savage winds and a storm that battered the town. Books were destroyed, manuscripts were torn, pages flew away, and nasty raindrops dissolved the ink. Stories were being lost forever.

Alodie had to put an end to it, but she wasn't a fighter. She used words, she argued, she reasoned. Although how does one reason with the one who hates words? How does one argue with the one who loves ignorance?

Alodie and Zyler stood in the main square facing each other. Inkwellers surrounded them, barely breathing,

merely waiting. The heavy grey clouds closed in on the whole town.

Zyler was quick to attack first. She threw a hurtful gust of wind to Alodie who fell to the ground. As she rose, Zyler hurled another blast of cold air. The sorceress showed no mercy. Alodie dodged Zyler's next blast and quickly made her way up. She raised her right hand and pronounced with a dauntless voice:

> *Hail to the Guardian Words of yore*
> *Masterly and powerful, they cut like a sword*
> *Immortal and patient, through time they remain*
> *They cannot be silenced, forever they'll reign*
> *By the wisdom of the Watchful Sages*
> *I tie thy will to harm through all the ages.*

Zyler fainted to the ground. Alodie closed her eyes and when she opened them again she saw the town celebrating. Inkwell was safe once again.

Alodie's enchantment took all of Zyler's powers away. The swish of her cape lost all might. The blow of her breath lost its sorcery. Clemens flew away, scared and alone, never to be seen again. The writers of Inkwell then decided to send Zyler to live inside the Wide Woeful Tree in the darkest part of the Wood of Whispering Weeping Willows.

The enchantment had left the sorceress weak and flimsy, almost as transparent as a sheet of tracing paper, but she wasn't so weak as to give up her meanness. Imprisoned in the Wide Woeful Tree, she plotted her revenge. She spent days and nights thinking and scheming, perfecting her evil plan. She barely slept. Years passed and became decades. Those wore on and turned to centuries. Until one night, one unruffled night with a waning half-moon, she found the loophole. She raised her arms and roared:

When there are no eyes around
When the moon welcomes no sound
My evil Pox, I summon thee
One imp to quell from A to Z.

The First Message

It was already dark when Florence, Grandpa Davey and Ben returned to the cottage. Outside only a few animals were heard walking, their footsteps crunching in the frosted grass. A musky night breeze made the branches rattle easily and a drip of melting snow ticked like a clock's second hand.

They'd brought *Lacuna Lares* with them. The book was too important to be left in the bookshop, even if it could remain locked in the cabinet. Besides, there was still a lot of information missing and the book might help them again.

Grandpa Davey made tomato-potato sandwiches and hot chocolate. It was his belief that a happy stomach spread happiness to the heart, a happy heart then calmed the mind and one could think more clearly. Ben drank his hot chocolate in one of Grandma's thimbles. They ate in silence, mulling on all the events of the day.

It was Florence who finally spoke.

"Ben's in trouble, isn't he? He's the bookmark upon whom the spell was cast."

"I think so, yes," Grandpa Davey answered. "Pox renders Ben defenceless and he, the imp, does everything his master Zyler wishes him to do. And what she wants is to destroy our language."

"So Zyler is the schemer behind it all," Ben said. His voice was tight.

"Yes, she is," said Florence. "Because of Alodie's enchantment, Zyler couldn't touch any book, so a bookmark was the perfect solution."

"I'm not sure I understand," Ben said.

"Think about it," Florence explained. "Bookmarks are the only ones inside a book when human beings aren't watching. The books are unguarded and at the mercy of the imp."

"The spell mentions the moon, what does that mean?" Ben asked.

"Good question," Grandpa Davey said as he poured more hot chocolate into the cups and thimble. "Let's see, the first time Pox took over Ben was…"

"On the Friday of December's waning half-moon," Florence ended the sentence without a trace of doubt.

"And the second time was yesterday, when the night sky was black," Grandpa Davey said.

"December's new moon," Florence said.

"So Pox appears every time the moon changes phases?" Ben asked.

"It makes sense. The moon has a huge power over everything. It's our closest celestial neighbour. In many ways, it affects the Earth, the tides, us humans. The moon's strong pull acts on every living thing on the planet. And what Zyler lacks is precisely that: strength. She was left too weak after Alodie's enchantment," Grandpa Davey said.

"That means the next time the moon changes phases, it's going to happen again," Florence said.

"A crescent half-moon. That's this Friday, only five days away," Grandpa Davey said.

"We need to find the solution to this before then! Otherwise I will be taken over by Pox again!" Ben cried. "I'm scared, Florence! Who knows what he'll do next time? Ay, ay, ay… The situation is already terrible as it is!"

"And we have to find a way to reverse all the damage that has already been done," Florence said. She was now thinking aloud. "So this is what we know so far: Zyler cast a spell upon Ben so that Pox would come to life every seven nights and little by little make sure we are left without words, because the worst of it all is that each time Pox is summoned by Zyler, his evilness seems to increase."

"But how did Pox do all that damage last night?" Ben asked.

"An imp is a supernatural creature," Florence said. "Pox can move at an unnatural speed, ignoring the laws of nature. He can appear and disappear at will. He's driven by a ravenous appetite for havoc. He must have jumped out of *The Adventures of Tom Sawyer* and gone into the world, wrecking every book he found along his way."

"But how?" Grandpa Davey asked.

"I don't know," Florence answered. "He must have said something to the words to make them want to run for their lives. Whatever it was, he managed to make stories disappear."

"Hide and seek," Ben whispered.

"What did you say?" Florence asked.

"I don't remember much from last night, as I said, it was all such a blur, but I do remember hearing those three words."

"He made the words play hide and seek," Grandpa Davey said. "And with that he was able to tamper with every book he could track down. And when there were no more of those, he just meddled with any piece of writing he stumbled upon, making the words play his game."

"One little imp with one simple game to ruin one of the greatest gifts humankind was ever given," Florence said.

For a while nobody said anything. The kitchen was completely still. The only movement came from the steam that trailed up from the pot of hot cocoa.

"How come everybody forgot about Zyler in the Wide Woeful Tree?" Ben asked.

It was Grandpa Davey who volunteered a theory. "I guess that people simply forgot. They locked the problem up inside the tree and preferred not to look that way. But nothing good comes out of locking a problem away. It doesn't solve anything. That being said, I also think sometimes good people tend to underestimate the evil nature of some creatures. Maybe no one thought Zyler would work so hard to keep doing harm."

"Maybe," Ben said, nodding in agreement.

ରୁ

The three of them walked up the uneven staircase. They thought it best if Ben didn't sleep inside *The Adventures of Tom Sawyer*, at least for the moment. There was a bitter omen in sleeping amid written chaos. Grandpa Davey made a bed for Ben with an empty matchbox filled with cotton. Then he went to his bedroom and put on his pyjamas and his comfy sleep cap.

After a few hours, everyone was asleep but Florence. She was worried for Ben. If only she could help him and set him free from the spell. Despite staring through the window without making the slightest noise, her heart was trembling with wariness. The wariness that comes from not knowing an answer.

Florence squeezed her eyes shut. She had never felt this restless before. She knew this was not only about Ben; it was also about the books and the words in them. The world had changed because of Zyler's plan. Stories were lost. Many tales and traditions had ceased to exist. Written accounts of past events were gone and hundreds of other stories were not going

108

to be inspired because of this. The thread of inspiration that had begun thousands of years ago was now torn. She made an effort not to hold on to that thought since it was too dreadful to bear. As it always happened when there was sadness in her heart, Florence's eyes had turned deep green, for the colour of her eyes couldn't help but follow her spirit.

She grabbed the hand-knitted blanket, wrapped it around her and went downstairs. The living room was utterly still and quiet. She had never been awake this late at night. She felt like a grown-up in the dark silence.

She sat on the sofa and glanced at *Lacuna Lares*. The book rested on the coffee table. It looked so big she felt intimidated by it, but as she came nearer she heard a call coming from it. It was as if the book wanted to be read by her at that exact moment, in that precise place.

She brought it closer to her and opened it. She flipped through it carefully. The pages were once again blank. She turned over one page, then another, and three more after that. She skimmed through the empty pages. Her browsing gradually turned to perusing and then to scanning the bare, clean sheets.

She was just about to give up and close the book when she remembered something her grandfather had once said to her: "*You'll jump all the fences and never fall apart, if you trust your senses and come what may follow your heart.*"

She decided to keep turning the pages. And although words were nowhere to be seen in *Lacuna Lares*, she kept going, scouting every centimetre of every page. But it was only when she stopped looking so hard and simply admired the beauty of the old pages gone brown round the edges that she realized the call had become a pulsing thump, like the beating of a drum. She sniffed and noticed the scent of hidden stories and secret tales that wanted to be revealed. It was then that she saw something on the open page before her:

Florence.

Soon more words popped up:

Bloom, blossom, flowering soul. That's the meaning of your name. Become who you are meant to be. Do not surrender yourself to melancholy. Make language flourish again. Go see the one who sews time and measures hours.

A

Did A stand for Alodie? Was that a message from the Word-Keeper? What did it mean? Who was she supposed to become? Florence went over these questions, hopping from one to the other, trying to figure out the answers.

She slowly flipped the pages of *Lacuna Lares* to see if there was any clue to what it all meant, but nothing else popped up. She read and re-read the message. The night rolled by as Florence's brain kept going over the message and the questions that had sprung from it.

The sky was beginning to clear and Florence's battering eyelashes were saying "*Go to sleep!*" She lay back on the sofa and closed her eyes but she could still see the questions floating around in her head. She tried counting binary numbers because that was her foolproof remedy: *One... One, zero... One, one... One, zero, zero... One, zero, one... One, one, zero... One, one, one... One, zero, zero, zero...* Nothing. Not even binary numbers worked this time.

Then something calmed her down. Florence let that feeling embrace her. It was as if there was someone right there by her side whispering lullabies. She began to let go of the questions, one at a time, and slowly fell asleep on the living room sofa.

The Box

Florence woke up to the smell of cinnamon buns, meringue mushrooms and chamomile tea. Grandpa Davey and Ben were making breakfast. In the light of day, things always looked better. It was as if the sun brought little sparkles of hope and problems looked easier to fix than during the dark hours of the night.

She rubbed her eyes, combed her hair with her hands and walked to the kitchen. She peeped round the door and saw Ben running all over the kitchen counter fetching ingredients for Grandpa Davey and trying to learn the recipes at the same time. She liked watching them. For a moment, she felt there was nothing wrong in their lives. But just like a bubble bursts when it touches something other than air, she remembered Zyler and Pox and was brought back to reality without warning.

"Good morning," she said at last.

"Good morning!" Grandpa Davey and Ben replied at the same time.

"How did you sleep?" the former asked.

"Quite well…though something happened last night."

Grandpa Davey and Ben stopped what they were doing and jerked their heads around.

"No, no, it was nothing terrible," Florence clarified quickly. "It was just something…strange."

Grandpa Davey and Ben hurried with the breakfast,

brought it to the table and listened to Florence's anecdote from the night before. When she was done, Grandpa Davey sighed with relief. "Well, isn't this remarkable! A message from the Word-Keeper herself! Can I take a look at it?"

"Of course," Florence answered. She went to the living room and came back with *Lacuna Lares* in her hands. She placed it on the kitchen table. Grandpa Davey moved his cup of chamomile tea, brought the book closer to him, put on his reading glasses and read the message out loud.

"Aaawesssome!" Ben said with a booming, warped voice. He gulped down the huge bite of meringue mushroom he was chewing, received a lively cheer from Grandpa Davey for making a horrendous swallowing sound, and asked, "But who's *the one who sews time and measures hours*'?"

"A clockmaker," Florence answered.

"Mr Tickery," Grandpa Davey said.

"Who's Mr Tickery?" Ben asked.

"He's Inkwell's clockmaker," Grandpa Davey answered.

"I've never met him," Florence said, looking at her grandfather. "I've heard of him, and I've walked past his cottage several times, but I've never actually met him."

"He keeps a lot to himself. He seldom leaves his cottage, which is in fact his factory, and it has been like that for as long as I can remember," Grandpa Davey said. He finished his cup of tea and then added, "We should go see him at once."

"No," Florence said, "I will go see him. Alodie's message was for me. This is something I have to do on my own. You should go to the main square and tell the town everything we've found out so far. They need to know what we're up against."

Grandpa Davey was about to say, "I can't let you go alone, I'll come with you!" but instead he bit his lip, nodded and said,

"I'll do that. I'll tell everyone what's happened in Inkwell, and I'll make sure *Lacuna Lares* remains safe." Then he watched as his granddaughter left the cottage on her own.

℅

Mr Tickery was Inkwell's meticulous, perfectionist and patient clockmaker. He was a master craftsman who built clocks by hand. Even though Florence had never met him, she'd heard time and time again that he was a timepiece wizard.

He lived on Roman Road in a little cottage that looked like a giant cuckoo clock. As a matter of fact, the round dormer window in the front of the house opened every day at noon and two robins came flying out to sing all around town, informing everyone that the first half of the day was over. At midnight, it was the turn of a couple of nightingales, and their heart-warming voices, to let Inkwell know the day had ended.

Florence knocked on the door. She heard footsteps approaching from inside the house. She stood straight and tucked her hair behind her ears. A tiny old man with tiny round spectacles and bushy, unruly eyebrows greeted her.

"Florence Ibbot, I've been expecting you. Please, come in."

"You've been expecting *me*?"

"Yes, I have. I've been waiting for you for a very long time," he answered with a casual voice that had a hint of secrecy.

"But we didn't have an appointment, did we?" Florence asked.

"No, we didn't."

"And…we've never met."

"No, we haven't."

"I see, so you know me through my granddad? Davey? He must have told you about me," Florence said, expecting Mr Tickery to agree to her deduction.

"No, not really." The tiny old man shook his head. "We've

113

never met and your grandfather didn't tell me about you. That doesn't contradict the fact that I've been expecting you."

"Aha, I understand," Florence said without really understanding. She looked at Mr Tickery and his eyes seemed to tell her he knew too much about her. He waved her in and showed her the way to his little factory inside the house.

A confused Florence followed Mr Tickery to a room crammed with clocks: little ones, big ones, old ones, wooden ones, marble ones. Florence felt dizzy at the sight of so many timepieces. Sundials, hourglasses, long-case clocks and pocket watches. He even had a big rusty round clock from the Old Arcane train station. They all seemed to be ticking together, making a very precise rhythm.

"This *ti-ki-ti-tak* sound helps me think straight when I have to work," Mr Tickery told Florence. He sat on a stool next to his working table. Then he offered Florence another wooden stool to sit on.

"I'm not sure why I'm here," she said, still a bit dazed by her surroundings.

"I am."

"You are?"

"Alodie's message."

"How do you know about that?"

"A long time ago she asked me to create something for you and give it to you today."

"You knew Alodie?"

"Indeed I did."

She wondered how old Mr Tickery was but she had once been told by a teacher at school never to ask that question to an older person. Florence had never really understood the reason behind this rule of conduct.

"It's impolite, Florence!" the teacher had preached.

114

"Why would it be impolite?" Florence had asked her.

"It just *is*," was the teacher's answer.

It wasn't a well-founded answer according to Florence but she decided not to pursue the matter any further. To the best of her knowledge, there was nothing wrong with age. A person could be two or eight or twenty-eight or eighty-two, what the difference was, she didn't know. Every age was good for its own reasons.

Be that as it may, she decided not to ask Mr Tickery how old he was. What's more, there were other questions that came hurtling against one another that Florence was certain were more important.

"Where is Alodie now? What happened to her? Why did she disappear?" she asked in a span of three seconds.

"Little by little, human beings, absorbed in their busy lives, lost their ability to interact with genies. Men forgot they were there. So one day genies decided to go back to their own universe. As for Alodie, she did the same after the final encounter with Zyler. Abelard, her faithful companion, tagged along and off he went with her. And the thing is, once a genie goes back to her realm, she can never come back here to Earth." He paused, doubting if he should say what he said next. "However, the great knowledge genie she was, Alodie didn't leave without first making sure that if something ever were to happen, there would be someone to take her place."

"Who... Me?"

Mr Tickery nodded.

"No, no, no... You probably have me confused with someone else."

"No, I don't think so."

"No, no, no, no, no," Florence repeated and then went ahead and added a few more noes because five just didn't seem enough to let the clockmaker know how wrong he was. "No, no, no, this has to be a mistake."

"No, it's not," Mr Tickery answered.

"But I'm a girl. I'm not a genie," Florence argued.

"I know that. You don't need to be a genie to care for words," Mr Tickery argued back.

"I wouldn't know how to do this. I'm only eleven years old!"

"Life is the most perfect clock ever created. It runs error free, always on the dot. Everything happens precisely when it has to happen."

When he finished uttering that sentence, the clock that was hanging right behind Florence stopped ticking.

"Ah, see what I mean? It is time," Mr Tickery said. He stood up and with the slowest of walks went to the back of the room and brought back something with him. With a shaking, wrinkled hand, he handed Florence a small case in the shape of a cube made of wood and copper.

"Alodie asked you to make this for me?" Florence asked.

"Yes, she did," Mr Tickery answered.

"Is there something in it? How do I open it?" Florence asked.

"That's for you to discover, for you are now the keeper of the box and everything it holds inside."

The Chocolatier's Tale

Florence decided to take a walk around Inkwell before heading back to Grandpa Davey's cottage. She was holding the box in her hand and too many thoughts in her head. The main one being: the clockmaker was wrong. All this had to be a mistake. She couldn't possibly be the one to replace Alodie. She decided she wasn't going to tell anyone about it. What Mr Tickery had said about her was clearly inaccurate.

Things seemed to be going awry and the answer to the whole lousy trouble kept getting knocked further away. Florence felt a bit puzzled. But since she liked puzzles, she then figured it was not such a bad feeling to have. She just had to unpuzzle herself out of that situation, and a good old-fashioned string of logical thoughts seemed like a reasonable way to do that.

"What would be the first thing to do now?" she asked herself.

"I have to find a way to open the box," she answered herself. She couldn't just break it. It was a present. One doesn't break presents, especially if it was a present that someone had made specially for her.

The first step towards solving the whole lousy trouble was taken. "That wasn't so hard," she thought. However, things were not always as easy as they seemed. Sometimes logical thoughts got tangled with emotions such as fear and heartache, and Florence was feeling both of those things. That made everything blurry and blue again.

As she walked down Rhetorical Road, Florence saw that the town looked deserted. The main square was empty and the maple tree was all alone in the stillness of the afternoon. Everyone was inside their cottages. Florence reckoned that most of them were probably lamenting the disaster that had fallen upon them; others were maybe too afraid of the imp and didn't even want to set a toe outside their homes. As she turned the corner of Colophon Drive, Florence passed by Percival's cottage. Through the main window of his cottage, she saw that Percival kept trying to find the rhyme that had disappeared from his poems. He looked everywhere: inside the kitchen cupboards, underneath the mattress, inside every bush in his garden. But he found nothing: the rhyme was definitely nowhere in his house.

When she crossed Pulp Lane, and walked through Inkwell's Library, Florence witnessed that Lorelai was doing her best to put some order in there, but it looked as if an angry tornado had passed through it. Once she got to Longhand Street, Florence saw how Imogen was trying to remember some of the stories the imp had destroyed so she could illustrate them. But she was so sad that tears rolled down her cheeks and fell onto the paper, blurring the lines of her drawings.

Florence didn't see Ignatius when she walked past his cottage on Tale Street. She figured he was most likely locked up in his laboratory trying to develop some kind of device to unscramble the words. But this was outside his area of expertise and no apparatus he could make would be able to put the words in order again or make them come out of hiding.

As soon as she got to Afterword Street, she spotted Mr McGlue on his front lawn. He was working hard to mend the books, that was his craft after all. But the pile of torn books was too high. Not to mention that many of the words were lodged in the spines. He was using tweezers to pluck them out but the words were too fragile and would break if he pulled too hard.

"Hi, Mr McGlue," Florence said.

He looked up. "Even if I could mend the books, I can't do anything about the words that are still mixed up. Am I trying to mend the unmendable, Florence? What good is a book without words?"

Florence didn't answer, and with grief-stricken hands, Mr McGlue continued his attempt to salvage at least one book.

She decided to head home down Fable Avenue. She was deeply in thought, holding the box in her two hands, when she walked by the chocolatier's shop. In a wavelike dance the smell of warm chocolate came flying out of the shop and went straight into Florence's nostrils. Before she realized, her stomach was making growling sounds. She popped inside the shop.

Monsieur Pépite was a tall, slim man with a homely face. He had a pointy chin and a taut mouth roofed with a long, thin moustache whose tips were always thrust up. He had come to Inkwell all the way from the Alps and he spoke with an acute French accent. Every now and then he liked to tuck French words into whatever he was saying.

He was standing behind the counter, holding a bowl with one hand and stirring its contents with a wooden spoon. He heard Florence coming in and looked up.

"Welcome, *Mademoiselle* Florence," he said with a feeble voice.

"Hello, Monsieur Pépite," Florence replied politely.

"Would you like a chocolate cupcake with a melting fudge heart, *chéri*?" the chocolatier asked. "It's the only recipe

I know by heart. So it's the only thing I've been able to bake ever since my book of recipes got scrambled up."

A chocolate cupcake with a melting fudge heart seemed to be the perfect baking expression of Florence's current state of mind. If her emotions were to become an edible thing, it would have been one of those cupcakes, so she gently said, "I'd love to try one."

Monsieur Pépite chose the prettiest cupcake he could find and handed it to her.

"*Voilà, Mademoiselle* Florence, *bon appétit!*"

She took a bite and giggled without even noticing she was giggling.

"It's the chocolate," Monsieur Pépite said. "It has a supreme power to make you happy when you eat it, that's why I love my craft so much. I'm a bringer of happiness. And as irony would have it, that's why I'm so sad and baffled that I've lost all my recipes."

"I know something about being sad and baffled," Florence said. "You feel deflated, like a used balloon."

"Exactly, like a *glubottant*," Monsieur Pépite said.

"What a fantastic word. Though I don't really know what it means. Is it French?" Florence said, furrowing her eyebrows.

"No, it's not French. A *glubottant* is an exploded balloon," the chocolatier said. "It's one of the many words a magical being once created."

"A creator of words? How cool is that? Who was this being?"

"It was one of the stories my nanny used to tell me when I was a little boy before I went to sleep. When I lived in the Alps, I had an English nanny. She was the one who taught me English and she used to read me stories every night before I went to bed. But this particular story was not in a book. My nanny knew it by heart and she told it with the softest voice."

"Would you mind telling it to me?"

"Of course I wouldn't mind. In fact, now that I think about it, it was one of my favourite bedtime stories. It was a fairytale about this blue-haired genie who created words and watched over our language."

Florence suddenly knew it was not just a fairytale. The chocolatier's nanny was talking about Alodie. This couldn't be a coincidence.

"What else did your nanny tell you about this genie?"

The chocolatier began reminiscing about his forgotten bedtime tale. "It was many years ago. I'm not sure I can remember all that well… *Bon, alors*, let's see." Monsieur Pépite closed his eyes as if this gesture would help him remember. "Ahhh… *Oui, oui, oui*, it's coming back to me now… As the fairytale goes, this blue-haired genie was truly *magnifique!* She had been around when extraordinary events had happened in the world. She'd been present more than two thousand years ago when epic stories were told. She'd breezed in when troubadours performed their stories of chivalry and courtly love. She was there when writers grabbed their pens to write their *romans*. She had appeared whenever a composer was struggling to discover the right melody for a symphony. And she'd been by the side of poets as they found the perfect word to end their villanelles."

When he finished his story, the chocolatier had a faraway look. He seemed to be miles away.

"Are you alright, Monsieur Pépite?"

"I was just thinking how *merveilleux* it would be if there really existed a genie that devoted her entire life to ridding the world of ignorance."

Inside Scriptoria Hill

The clockmaker's box had what looked like a very peculiar keyhole. Florence had tried every key she'd found with no happy results. She spent hours trying to find a clue about how to open the box. Since all the books were useless, she tried to remember everything she'd read to see if anything might help, from history books to old myths and fables. From what she could recall, none of them mentioned a wood and copper box. She then turned to detective stories and tried to follow the deductive logic all great detectives in literature followed to solve mysteries. When that didn't work, she went to see Lorelai at the Inkwell Library.

"What can I do for you this morning, Florence?"

"I'm looking for manuals on how to open locked things. Were there any books left unscrambled, Lorelai?"

"I'm sorry, darling. I don't think so. But I still haven't gone through all of the aisles. Check over there, in that aisle to your left, see if you can find anything that might be of help."

"Thanks, Lorelai."

Florence found a couple of old handbooks to open safes, but as Lorelai had predicted, they were all unreadable. It was impossible to follow any of the instructions.

ɛɔ

The ash tree in Grandpa Davey's garden had finally lost all its leaves. The two sheep wandered around the yard completely unfazed by the cold weather. Inside the cottage, Grandpa Davey was piling up logs in the fireplace. Ben stood on the coffee table, waiting to see how Grandpa Davey started the fire.

Florence sat on her bed. "I'm nowhere near finding an answer to this," she said while looking at the clockmaker's box. "I could really use some good advice now…" It was Mr Rook who popped up in her head. Why was she suddenly thinking about her chess teacher? She made a mental list of all the things he'd taught her to see if any could come in handy.

"*Evaluate your position.*"

Florence thought of all the events that had led to this moment: making her annual trip to Inkwell, creating Ben, choosing *The Adventures of Tom Sawyer*, visiting Mr Tickery, reading *Lacuna Lares*. Then she thought of Alodie and Zyler. That made her remember the moon and she realized there was little time left till the next change of the moon phase. She put that thought on hold and kept going through Mr Rook's chess lessons.

"*Consider the safety of the king.*"

She thought of *Lacuna Lares*. The book needed to be kept safe. So did Ben.

"*Remember all the different types of attacks and defences.*"

Florence tried to come up with a game plan to strike Zyler and Pox. An idea began to take form in her mind, though she couldn't altogether grasp it yet.

"*What are your opponent's threats?*"

Mr Rook had told Florence that she needed to ask herself this question before every game. Her answer this time: Zyler was shattering human language to pieces. What greater threat was there?

"*What are the consequences of your opponent's last move?*"

A world where words don't know their place, and if words

don't know that, there's little we can do with them.

"Look for the smartest move and think five steps ahead."

She closed her eyes and followed Mr Rook's advice. Then she ran downstairs, grabbed her hooded poncho, asked Ben if he wanted to go with her and together they left the cottage at once.

∽

Florence had deduced that the next reasonable move was to go visit Hephy. Why hadn't she thought of her before? She hadn't even visited her yet. She would always go see her as soon as she got into town but this year things had been different.

Hephy was Inkwell's blacksmith. Her hair was of bright intense yellow and she always had it styled in a messy and sooty fishtail plait. She was tough, hard-working and, because her hands and cheeks were usually covered in black smudges, few people saw how strikingly gorgeous she was.

She dwelled inside Scriptoria Hill. Not as high as a mountain, but just as rocky, Scriptoria Hill was a chocolate-coloured hill that stretched above a green meadow to the north of Inkwell, just below the Towering Mountains of the East. It had stood there for centuries. Its rough steep slopes climbed up towards the sky and ended in an open saw-toothed peak, for Scriptoria Hill was in fact a small volcano where Hephy forged all her craft.

She rarely stepped outside the hill. She preferred to stick to her metalworking. She used her tools to make gates, candleholders, cauldrons, brass rings for the merry-go-rounds, and although other blacksmiths made weapons, she never did. What she did forge were keys. Florence needed her skills. She was no ordinary blacksmith. Her finely wrought metalwork was faultless and it was held in great respect by those who knew the craft.

Inside Scriptoria Hill it was dark and sizzling hot. As Florence and Ben walked inside the volcano, the temperature grew higher. Ben walked beside her. His hands and face were muggy. He didn't like it in there and found himself wishing he were in Florence's bedroom, smelling cinnamon and sonnets. But he didn't say anything for he reckoned he had to remain strong.

Florence was suddenly overwhelmed by the heat waves. She could barely breathe and could taste nothing but the sultry air. But she knew it wasn't just the heat that was nagging her. *Is this a hopeless quest? Am I brave enough to do this? What if I can't save the words? How will I face Zyler? What if she wins?* These were the doubts that made it difficult for her to walk. All these wretched fears were smothering her. She was angry and her eyes had turned to the deepest shade of gun-metal grey.

She stopped walking and stood still in the middle of the cave in the volcano. Ben stopped right after her.

"Florence? What's wrong?" he asked.

She remained silent, staring down at the ground. Her eyes were filled up with tears and she began to cry without making the slightest sound.

In her head, she yelled to her doubts and fears, "I don't want you here!" but that was the point: they were *hers*. They weren't someone else's doubts and fears. They were Florence Ibbot's. Only she could dispose of them.

"Please, leave! Please!" she begged. But they wouldn't, because the thing with doubts and fears is that they don't leave out of their own free will. They tend to cosy up in the mind who chooses them and they are bad tenants. They are noisy and they never let you forget they are there. It's up to the owner to kick them out.

Florence remembered what her grandfather did with

his doubts: he fried them, made French toast out of them and ate them with maple syrup. She couldn't do that now, in the middle of a volcano. Instead she decided to grab all her doubts and fears by their tail, spin them till they whizzed and toss them into the darkness of the cave. It was hard. Those doubts and fears wanted to cling on to her like a tick, sucking all hope only to grow larger. Beads of sweat appeared on her forehead as she struggled to grab those stinking feelings by their tail and out of her heart.

Once she succeeded, she managed to hurl them away with such a force she didn't even see where they landed. After she'd shaken them off completely, she quickly replaced them with good thoughts: salted hazelnuts in brown paper bags, warm milk with tons of honey, lumpy mashed potatoes with nutmeg, long chess games with Mr Rook, Melvin's riddles, the bell on the entrance door of the bookshop, Grandpa Davey's fruit pizza, Grandma Winifred's really long scarves, and her favourite word: *pamplemousse*. Florence's eyes had now shifted to the brightest golden amber.

She turned to Ben. "OK, we can keep going now."

"Florence, what did you just do?"

"I've just learned something."

"What do you mean? When? Just now?"

"Yes, just now."

"So if you learned it a minute ago that means you learned it on your own."

"It seems I did, yes."

"That's a good way to learn something."

"It was more like a sudden revelation."

"A sudden revelation?"

"Yes, like an insight."

"An epiphany you could say."

126

"You could definitely say an epiphany because that's what it was."

"What about?"

"How to get rid of my doubts and fears."

"Good for you. Can you teach me?"

And as they resumed their walk, Florence taught Ben all about Grandpa Davey's frying technique and her whizzing by the tail one.

Hephy

As they kept going deep inside the passageways of Scriptoria Hill, they began to hear the crackling of flame and the hammering on steel. They came to an opening within the path and entered a huge maroon cavern. It was the centre of the volcano and there was Hephy smelting metallic ores.

The light of the fire made her eyes look spellbinding. She was heating pieces of iron until they became red-hot and soft enough to be shaped. There were anvils, chisels and all sorts of welding devices lying around.

"Hello, Hephy!" Florence said in a loud voice, trying to be heard over the sounds of hissing steam and the grinding rasp of metal against a granite sharpening wheel. Hephy stopped what she was doing and looked up. A smile flickered across her lips. She put the hammer down and ran across the smithy.

"Flo! Hi!" she said as she gave Florence a big hug without realizing she was getting her all dirty with charcoal.

"It's so good to see you, friend. It's been too long!" Florence said as she shook the charcoal off with a swift jiggle.

From the corner of her eye, Hephy saw a chubby little creature, standing straight as a soldier about to salute, extending his tiny hand. "What in the name…?" Hephy's eyes grew wider and ceased blinking as she watched the bookmark in front of her.

Florence quickly introduced them. "Hephy, this is Benjamin, my bookmark."

128

Hephy glanced at Florence and then at Ben who was still extending his tiny hand. Florence began to further explain herself.

"Well, of course! Why was I so surprised?" Hephy said when Florence was done with the story. "If anyone could do this, it would be you."

"I didn't even know I could," Florence said.

"This definitely tops the beanie hat that takes away bad dreams," Hephy said.

"He certainly does," Florence said, winking her long black eyelashes at Ben. Then she finished the introduction. "Ben, this is Hephy, my best and oldest friend in the world, and Inkwell's renowned blacksmith."

"Delighted to meet you," said Ben, who had blushed a little bit when he saw, now closer to her, how beautiful the blacksmith was.

"Nice to meet you too, Ben," Hephy said.

Florence and Hephy told Ben how Florence would always visit her in Scriptoria Hill. They always spent the winters together. And it had been like that since they were little.

"Sometimes I just go to Inkwell and we hang around in the main square," Hephy said.

"Or you stay with us at the cottage for a few days, right?" Florence said.

"That's mainly because of your grandfather's awesome cooking," Hephy said.

"Ha ha, funny," Florence said.

"Jokes aside, I wish Florence didn't live in the city. But… that's the way it is," Hephy said.

"How do you know when you've found your best friend?" Ben asked them.

"It's quite simple," Florence said. "I'm happy if a happy

thing happened to Hephy and Hephy is sad if I'm going through a tough time."

"And Florence teaches me about books," Hephy said, "and I teach her about metals. We are always proud of each other's accomplishments and admire the best qualities in one another."

"I guess anything less than that isn't really a friendship. Think of it like this: it's the complete opposite to the Quarrelsome Queens," Florence said.

"Who are they?" Ben asked.

"Right, I haven't told you about them yet. Tabitha, Tallulah and Luella. They are these three girls in my school that… Well, they will never understand what a friend really is."

"Speaking of friendship, I was wondering what was taking so long for you to drop by this December!" Hephy said, throwing her arms up in the air.

"I know, I'm so sorry. I've been…delayed by some unfortunate events. Did you happen to hear anything about what happened in Inkwell?"

"No. I haven't been outside Scriptoria Hill in days. I've been working and you know what happens when I work… I just forget that there are hours or days or nights."

"I'll tell you about it in a second, but first tell me about you! How's everything in Scriptoria Hill? What are you making today?"

"A helmet. It's for Ignatius, so he stays protected when he's trying out his dicier inventions."

"That's clever," Florence said.

"And what's your favourite piece to make?" Ben asked her.

"Hmm, that's a tough question. I like making railings, but cooking utensils are also fun to make. Lately I've been doing some sculptures, but I don't think I can pick just one.

Everything I do has its own special meaning," Hephy said. "Isn't it the same for you and your books, Flo? Could you choose just one if you had to?"

"No, you're right, I don't think I could," Florence answered and closed her eyes to ease away the image of all the wounded books. Besides, she still hadn't said anything to Hephy about that matter.

Ben walked around the smithy looking over all the tools and gadgets Hephy had there. He tried to lift them up to see what they were for. No matter his determination and despite his noble intent, he soon worked out that lifting those tools wasn't a sensible plan. The pursuit of his goal might become catastrophic. So he stood back and appraised the tools and gadgets from a distance, crossing his arms, lifting his chin and raising one eyebrow.

Hephy and Florence, who were witnessing all this, couldn't help but laugh. Then Hephy turned to stoke the fire. "Oh, Flo, before I forget, I made something for you."

"You did?"

"I hope you like it," Hephy said as she handed a little felt bag to her friend.

Florence opened it and inside she found a chain-link necklace with a circle pendant. It had the name *Florence* etched around it. It was greyish-blue but it would wink an orangey gleam when turned slightly to either side. Hephy clasped it around Florence's neck. "I've poured a drop of pure fire in it. Keep it close to your heart, it has an ever-burning flame inside that will heighten your courage when you need it."

Florence looked at it and then looked at her friend. It was as if Hephy somehow knew she needed this. That was the thing with their friendship: sometimes words weren't even necessary.

They laughed about the time Florence created a lava flow while attempting to melt a big igneous rock she'd found inside Scriptoria Hill (incidentally, that was the day she got her nickname Flo), but things got more serious when Florence explained to Hephy most of what had happened over the past few days.

"We need your help to open this box," Florence said, showing her the gift Mr Tickery had given her.

"This is fine work," Hephy said. She held the box in her hand. "If you need what rests inside, I can help you open it." Then she looked at it again. "Oh…"

"*Oh?*" Ben said. "What does *Oh* mean? That didn't sound like a good *Oh*."

"I need to take a closer look," Hephy said. She walked to one of the corners of the smithy where there was a huge pile of scrap metal. She searched around it and pulled out a weird-looking bronze mono-goggle with a leather strap. She fastened it around her head and looked through the keyhole again. "Just like I suspected," Hephy said, shaking her head. "The key to open your gift needs to be made with *A'goo Egre*."

"With what?" Ben said.

"*A'goo Egre*," Hephy said.

"What's that?" Florence said.

"It was an extremely rare metal," Hephy said.

"Why did you use the past tense?" Florence said.

"Because it doesn't exist any more," Hephy said.

"What do you mean?" Ben said.

"In ancient times, you could find it everywhere, but it was so beautiful it was used in the most careless way. Everyone wanted something made of *A'goo Egre*. And when they had one thing made with it, they wanted another one, and then another one. So as you can imagine, it became scarce quite quickly.

Now it's been ages since anyone's seen it."

"But what happened to all the things made with it? Can't we use one of those to make the key?" Florence asked.

"Well, that's the thing. No one knew at the time that *A'goo Egre* vanishes with time. It slowly evaporates till there's nothing left. Nature sometimes likes to make beautiful things last only a moment in time. And wisely so."

"So what are we going to do now?" Ben asked.

"There is only one place where I think I could find some," Hephy said.

"Where?" Florence said.

"In Haymel," Hephy said.

"Where's that?" Ben asked.

"It's the deepest cave in Scriptoria Hill," Florence said.

"I haven't been down there since my first days as an apprentice. My master took me there for training," Hephy said. "The rarest metals and minerals hide in the walls of Haymel."

Florence looked at her with a concerned look. "I remember you told me about it once. You have to climb down Black Chasm to get there, Hephy."

"I know," Hephy said. "But it's the only way. If we're lucky, I might find some *A'goo Egre*. I need to get at least a good chunk to make the key. I'll have to take my drilling equipment."

"We'll go with you," Florence said.

"That's not a good idea, Flo," Hephy said. "The temperature down Black Chasm is terribly high and you need a special suit. I only have one."

"I can't let you go alone, Hephy," Florence said.

"You have to. Besides, this is Scriptoria Hill, it's my volcano. It won't hurt me."

"Piping hot lava and roasting fumes are no one's friend," Ben said.

134

"I'll be fine," Hephy said.

Hephy put on what looked like some sort of old-fashioned diving suit mixed with a firefighter's costume and a welder's uniform. The garment looked incredibly heavy. It came with sturdy boots and a pair of heat-resistant gloves which she secured to the sleeves. There was a utility belt around her waist from where at least a dozen gadgets hung.

"Good luck, Hephy," Florence said.

"I'll be back as soon as I can," Hephy said. She grabbed a copper helmet that featured a little window and locked it around her head. Then she left in search of *A'goo Egre*.

&

Ben and Florence waited in the smithy. Florence knew they didn't have much time left, but she also knew they had no other option. They sat near the granite sharpening wheel and looked at each other.

"What do we do now, Florence?"

"Wait."

"That's it?"

"Pretty much."

"It's hard to wait when there's nothing to do but wait."

"If we talk about something that has nothing to do with the box, time might fly by quicker."

"OK." Ben thought for a few seconds. "Tell me about these Quarrelsome Queens."

"Well, there's a subject that will take our minds off our troubles."

"Why do you say that? Are they mean?"

"The meanest."

"As mean as Zyler and Pox?"

"No, certainly not. But they are mean in a different way. Tabitha is the leader, and Tallulah and Luella follow her

135

everywhere. They think they rule the school, and they have everybody believe that, so in the end, I guess they do rule it."

"Can't you do something about it?"

"It's not that easy. I remember this one time when Netty, a girl in my class, lent Tabitha her brand new beaded bracelet. Tabitha promised she would give it back the next day, but needless to say, the bracelet ended up living in Tabitha's bedroom, soon to be forgotten among the other eighty-eight bracelets and bangles she owned. Netty was crushed when Tabitha said she'd accidentally lost the bracelet on her way home."

"Why? Why would she do such a thing?"

"Because there are people that just like to twist words."

"You mean lie and bamboozle and trick?"

"Yep."

"So what happened?"

"I was near them in the playground so I'd overheard what happened. I suspected Tabitha was probably lying so I went over there and told her to be careful."

"Careful of what?"

"When you use a word, you have to make sure you know what stands behind it. Words mean nothing without their meaning. They crack, like a broken eggshell, and it's very hard to mend a broken word. I told Tabitha that lying like that would eventually get her into trouble."

"What did she do when you said that?"

"She laughed in my face, of course, and she never gave Netty her bracelet back. That's the way they are."

"That's too bad. I'm sad for Netty though."

"I was too," Florence said and grabbed her green corduroy backpack. She took out a bottle of water and a tin can full of oatmeal cookies.

"Want one?" Florence asked.

"A tiny piece is enough for me."

"Right!" Florence said as she realized that Ben was barely bigger than a cookie.

After the snack, Florence dozed off, her head resting on the granite wheel. Ben climbed up her leg, got inside a pocket in her T-shirt and before he knew it, he was also fast asleep.

The Second Message

It took Hephy over eleven hours to come back from Haymel but for Florence and Ben it felt like eleven years.

"Did you find it?" Florence asked.

Hephy unhooked her helmet. "Climbing down Black Chasm wasn't too hard, but once I got to Haymel, things got complicated. I'd forgotten that the walls there are extremely brittle. I couldn't use my drilling gear. The sound made the whole cave tremble. So I had to do it by hand, with my mining pick. That's why it took me so long. I could barely see, it was so dark down there."

"Are you OK?" Florence asked.

"Yes, yes, I'm fine," Hephy answered.

"And…were you able to…?" Ben asked.

"I was," Hephy said. "I found the *A'goo Egre*."

She opened her hand. A roughly cut piece of colourless metal rested there, and even though it was transparent, it beamed its own silvery light.

"That's one of the most beautiful things I've ever seen," Florence said.

"It is, isn't it?" Hephy said.

"What now?" Ben said.

"Now, I'll get to work."

Inside Hephy's smelting house, one special key was forged by the hands of the skilful blacksmith. A small piece of shaped *A'goo Egre* with seven marks cut to fit the wards of that particular lock. How did Hephy know that seven marks were needed was a question that went without an answer. Florence didn't ask her, for she liked the mysterious ways in which her friend worked.

"Here," Hephy said as she handed Florence the key she'd forged. "This will unlock your box."

સ૦

Once outside Scriptoria Hill, the sun was shining. A big oak tree stood lonely on the side of a sloping hill. Its last shrivelled leaves swayed in the breeze and its branches drew gnarly shadows on the ground. Florence and Ben sat under it.

She opened her backpack and took out the bottle of fresh water and the tin can with the rest of the oatmeal cookies.

"What are those?" Ben said, pointing behind Florence. She turned around.

"Those are the Towering Mountains of the East."

"They are so high."

"All this land is fenced in by the Towering Mountains of the East, West, North and South. As far as I know, no one has ever reached their peaks."

"I bet the clouds have to go to the top of the sky to cross over them."

"Never thought about that, but I guess they do," Florence said as she shook the crumbs of an oatmeal cookie off her trousers. "Water?"

"No, thanks."

Florence took a swig from the bottle and then put it back in her backpack. She then grabbed the key Hephy had made and put the box in front of her. She looked at Ben.

"Are you ready?" she asked.

"I guess we have to be, right?"

139

"Right."

Florence placed the key inside the lock. She felt her heartbeat rising. She could hear it as well, just like when she was crossing the Farm Fields of Fleeting Feathers but much faster: *baboom-baboom-baboom-baboom-baboom*. Ben's face was frozen, as if staying still would somehow make time speed ahead to see what would happen in the next three seconds.

Florence turned the key and the four sides of the box opened like the petals of a blossoming rose. Within the box, there was a music box. As if activated by clockwork, a song started playing.

It was a song unlike any song they'd heard before. It was a charming waltz mixed with a military march mixed with some sort of sailor's shanty. The notes rose into the air, flying away in a glowing whirlwind. They flew above the oak tree and kept going up towards the mountains.

Moments later, a carrier pigeon came sliding through the clouds. He wore aviator goggles and had a messenger bag across his chest. He landed under the oak tree. Florence was fast to close the box. The music stopped.

"I've heard your call!" the carrier pigeon said with a bossy tone.

"What call?" Ben asked.

"The song from the music box, that was my call to come here. I must deliver a letter addressed to one Miss Florence Ibbot."

Florence and Ben looked at each other.

"I'm Florence Ibbot."

"You mean your name is Florence Ibbot," the bird clarified.

"Well, yes, I guess you're right, my name is Florence Ibbot."

"I *am* right, and I'm also a little bit late. I apologize. I don't like excuses but I come from very far away. As soon as I heard the melody from the music box, I departed with haste. But I was in the Caramel Way, which in case you don't know is the quiet place in the skies where all us carrier pigeons rest when we are tired. It's quite an amazing place. It hovers over an orange mist, breathtaking really, and when one is resting in a breathtaking place, it's easy to lose track of time… But enough chattering. This envelope is for you, Miss Ibbot. My business here is complete. Off I go now. Good luck to you!"

The bird flew away. Florence looked down at the envelope she had in her hands and then with a swift motion, she opened it. There was a note inside. She unfolded it.

"Another message signed with the letter A," she said.

"What does it say?" Ben asked.

"I can't read it," Florence said.

"What do you mean you can't? Why?"

"This has been written in the weirdest and loopiest calligraphy I've ever seen."

"A weird and loopy what?"

"Calligraphy. It's the art of writing beautifully," Florence said. "You could say it's the craft of creating a unique handwriting but sometimes, if one gets carried away, the letters become too knotty and almost impossible to read."

"So what do we do now?" Ben asked.

"We must go see Mr Caroling right away," Florence answered. "We don't have much time left. It's already Friday, so tonight's crescent half-moon will trigger the spell again. We can't let that happen."

※

Mr Caroling, the calligrapher, worked on Blackletter Lane, in a workshop that smelled of handmade paper and ink. Florence rang the bell and moments later the door squeaked opened.

"So sorry to disturb you at this hour, Mr Caroling," Florence said.

"No need to apologize, Florence. What can I do for you?"

"We need your help," Florence said. "It's really important."

"Your grandfather told us what's going on. Please, come in."

The three of them walked into the workshop and sat down around a big old desk.

Florence took the message out of her backpack and unfolded it in front of Mr Caroling.

"Can you tell us what this note says?" Florence asked.

Mr Caroling grabbed the piece of paper and studied it. "I've never seen this type of script before. A challenge this will be," he said. "But a challenge I will gladly accept."

Florence told him about their journey so far, just like she had done for Hephy. Mr Caroling told her that he'd heard the name of Alodie only once in his life, many years ago, when he was just a boy in school. It was a story his history teacher had told the class one foggy winter morning. He remembered his teacher's exact words because the tale did not sound at all like history but more like a fairytale.

"Once upon an ancient time there was a genie called Alodie. She was a warrior, but a different type of warrior from the ones you find in history books. She guarded language, knowledge and words without the use of muskets, spears or daggers.

"Great Word-Keeper that she was, she protected all the words, though she had a special fondness for the words that sounded delicious, like *butterscotch*, the weird and peculiar ones, like *behoove* or *astrolabe*, and the ones that made her

142

laugh; *moustache* and *collywobbles* were two of her favourites. She also loved the words that were hard to pronounce, like *abominable* and *miscellaneous*, the ones that she didn't get tired of pronouncing, like *doodle*, and the ones that lost their meaning when she repeated them out loud for too long, *ticket-ticket-ticket-ticket-ticket*. But then there were the ones she cherished the most…the words she made up.

"For indeed the Word-Keeper was a grand master at the art of wordsmithing. She had the skills to create words when necessary: *weephos*, for example, were the sneezes that got away and never came back; exploded balloons were *glubottants* and *grotalins* were the jokes one could never remember. She created a word for the days when one is clumsy all the time, *finpoon*, and *quinpees* were the days one met a good friend for the first time. *Aramooses* were the spontaneous trips and adventures, *loppies* were the clouds that looked like shredded cotton and *yucalies* were surprisingly disappointing dishes that made a person go 'ewww!' She crafted the word *oggiephant* for people who wore their glasses at the tip of their nose and the word *morsipog* for the person who wasn't able to listen to another human being."

"She was so much like you, Florence," Ben said.

"Indeed she was," Mr Caroling said, nodding. Florence didn't say anything. She remembered Mr Tickery's words and a tight knot gripped her heart.

Mr Caroling put on his glasses and hunched over his desk. Every once in a while, he got up and went to his library in search of old books and aged scrolls. He scratched his forehead often. He squinted and stooped his head over the piece of paper. He looked puzzled, then at ease, then clueless again, then worried, and finally pleased. When the last ray of sun left the horizon, Mr Caroling put his pen down and handed Florence the decoded message.

In a Wordless World

The sky grew heavier. The sun had sunk in the west and an unnatural stillness hovered over Inkwell. The haze of twilight brought about an earthy scent that scattered around every corner. Though still unseen, the moon was looming. Florence was about to read the message Mr Caroling had just handed to her when she became aware that Ben wasn't in the room.

"Where's Ben?" she asked.

"I don't know, I was zoomed in on my work… Oh no, look!" The calligrapher was pointing forward. The front door was ajar.

"Thank you for everything, Mr Caroling!" Florence said hastily and ran out of the workshop. Once outside, she looked all around. There was no sign of Ben on Blackletter Lane, nor on Rhyme Road, nor on Stanza Street. She made a fast decision to run down Allegory Alley.

"Ben! Ben! Where are you?" she cried out and darted across the town's main square. There was no response and Ben was nowhere to be seen. Florence looked up to the sky. A crescent half-moon was expected any minute now.

She hurried back to Grandpa Davey's cottage. She ran across the porch, across the living room and into the kitchen. While she caught her breath, she asked her grandfather if Ben was there.

"No, he's not," he replied.

"Are you sure?"

"Yes, of course I'm sure, I've been at the cottage all day. He didn't come back here," Grandpa Davey reassured her. "What happened? I thought you two were together."

"We were. We were at Mr Caroling's, but suddenly he was gone!" Florence said, panting. "I've looked all over Inkwell. I couldn't find him." She closed her eyes tight and whispered, "Ben, where are you? Where did you go?"

∞

Ben raced as fast as he could. "I was supposed to be the guardian of books and I've failed," he said. "I need to get as far away as possible from Inkwell. There's no other choice."

He reached the Wood of Whispering Weeping Willows. If you gave him a thousand years to ponder, he would never have said such a place could exist.

"What in the world is this? Where am I?"

He found no answers, only shadows that grew darker. He came to a rest and looked around. He saw it: the sorrow and heartache of the trees. He felt it: the melancholy, the agony and the pain. Ben was flooded with fear. He remembered what Florence had taught him in the caves of Scriptoria Hill. "Take your doubts and flip them by their tail or make French toast out of them." But when he tried to do so, he failed. Fear had iced him up from within and he'd become rooted to the teardrop-wet ground. His thoughts were clouded. He knew that to face his opponent he had to be tough, but he couldn't even breathe, let alone fling his doubts into the woods.

A crescent half-moon crept up the sky. Ben fell on his knees. The spell triggered the evil spark and Ben could feel the cold shivers swirl through his body. As the moon lit up the darkness of the woods, Pox took over him once more.

When the transformation was over, the imp raised his

head. His goggled eyes revealed nothing but scorn. He was carrying a crossbow in his hands and he flung his heavy tail this way and that. Without rush and with a big grin on his face, he turned on his heels and started making his way back to Inkwell.

༄

Back at the cottage, Florence closed both hands around a mug of hot cocoa. Its warmth eased her worry, if only just a little bit. She hadn't read the message yet. She was thinking where Ben could be; she was also filling Grandpa Davey in on all he'd missed but she knew she had to put all that aside and face the message.

She closed her eyes. She was still wearing Hephy's necklace and she felt the ever-burning flame inside the circle pendant near her heart. It didn't hurt. Just like Hephy had said, the drop of pure fire heightened Florence's courage. She held on tight to it. She opened her eyes and unfolded the piece of paper. Even though she'd never heard it before, she could almost listen to Alodie's voice as she began to read it. It was a silky voice with a note of wonder and a slight air of long-lost myth.

> Wield the words, not the sword. When you deal with words, you deal with the sharpest blade ever crafted. The realm of language belongs to you, not to her. I banned Zyler from doing harm once, but her spirit is evil. That dark seed has survived and feeds off Pox's evilness. It's gathering strength. You must defeat it. Succeed where I've failed. My spirit will guard you. Remember: it is only in the end that the beginning will arrive, when and if you find a way to make dawn and dusk hold hands.

Florence put the piece of paper down and looked up, her gaze fixed ahead. She felt it, a quiet inner jolt. It was invisible on the outside. It was happening deep inside of her. Something

146

withheld had been unfurled, as if the gates had been opened for an untamed horse to run free in the highlands, never to come back to the stable, free to gallop at its fastest pace.

"I know what I have to do," Florence said.

"How can I help you?" Grandpa Davey asked.

"The robins and the nightingales at Mr Tickery's house," Florence said. "We need their help."

They stepped outside the cottage but they weren't ready to see what they saw: a heart-wrenching massacre. Crossbow in hand, eyes on the sight, Pox was shooting not at the people of Inkwell, but at the words that had run out of the books while playing hide and seek. He was ruthless and his aim was unerring. The bolts whizzed past land and air and hit words into utter destruction.

"What's happened?" Grandpa Davey asked Mr McGlue.

"The imp stormed inside the library. We heard him shout something, couldn't really make out what he said, but then hundreds of words came dashing out of the building. That's when the shooting began," the bookbinder said.

Some Inkwellers had become stunned by fear. Others didn't move because they just didn't know what to do. A few hid behind trees or ran back to their homes to avoid getting hit by the bolts. "He can outrun and outflank us all!" someone cried. Pox moved too swiftly and was too skilful with his weapon. Without mercy, he kept butchering pieces of language.

Please was the first word to die and with it, good manners were gone and, out of the blue, everybody began to forget how to be polite. Then *promise* was killed and instantly people found it hard to remember the importance of commitments and pledges.

Pox didn't choose the words at random. He killed *honour*, not *shame*. He destroyed *victory*, but left *defeat* untouched. He executed *sincere*, but left *capricious* and *fickle* alive and well. He put *laughter* to death yet deliberately failed to hit *lament*. He shot down *freedom*, and didn't even touch *slavery*.

A few good words hid inside some not so good words. They had worked out Pox's strategy. The bad and ugly words provided perfect camouflage. That's how *one* hid inside *alone*, *here* snuggled inside *nowhere*, *eat* inside *sweat*, *cat* in *catastrophe* and *ace* inside *grimace*. They lay low there, without moving an inch or making a sound.

The moment Pox eliminated *why* from the human language, hundreds of questions were left unasked and unanswered. Everything became *ordinary* when the imp slaughtered the word *special* and *consequences* disappeared when *cause* was hit by one of the bolts.

Nothing seemed real when *truth* was killed. *Willpower* felt lost when it was left without *purpose*. When *light* was gone, no one knew what to call that brightness gifted by the sun, and in the absence of light, *darkness* began reigning. Pox then wiped out the word *safe* and panic spread all over Inkwell.

🙰

Florence rushed up Roman Road to Mr Tickery's house. When she reached the little cottage that looked like a giant cuckoo clock, she rested her hands on her knees and caught her breath. Then she called for the two robins and the two nightingales.

They came out the round dormer window at once and flew to her. Florence whispered something to them. The four birds answered with a simple nod, a nod that said they could handle the mission appointed to them and that they weren't going to let her down. They took to the air and fanned out.

As they soared away, the birds began to sing. Their birdsong caught the attention of everyone in town. Without words, the robins and the nightingales delivered Florence's message. The music fell like snowflakes and was heard all the way to the Towering Mountains of the West.

The Battle

The cold bit into Florence's face as they entered the Wood of Whispering Weeping Willows. All fellow Inkwellers marched together. Leading the frontline, Florence moved at a fast pace. One step at a time, they closed in on Zyler.

When Florence saw the ghostly mist ahead, she knew they were approaching the darkest part of the woods.

"I'm scared," Percival said.

"So am I," Imogen whispered.

"It's the sorrow of the trees. Find a good thing to think about. We're almost there," Florence told them.

"I can't find any," Percival said.

"Think about this: we'll fight a battle like no one has ever done it before," Florence said. "Keep repeating it, like a broken record."

ം

When they reached the Wide Woeful Tree, Pox was already there. He'd come to his master. He was holding his crossbow in one hand and a whole bunch of words in the other.

Florence turned around. Everyone was there. Not only Inkwellers, but also Melvin, all the inventors from the Riveting River Valley, the Feather Farmers, and having left all arrogance behind, the Pedantic Plum Trees had also travelled across the realm to join them in the dark woods.

"Where's Zyler?" Ignatius asked Florence.

"Still inside the tree," she answered.

"Florence! Watch out!" Hephy shouted and grabbed Florence by the shoulder to pull her down.

Pox had let the words loose. When they ran for their lives in all directions, he aimed and opened fire. Hephy's reaction was lightning fast. Slung over her back she had two shields. She clasped one on her left arm and tossed one to Florence. Though it was quite heavy, Florence caught it in mid-air and together they began stopping and diverting the bolts. They moved with the skill of two soldiers but Pox was shooting too fast.

Melvin and the game inventors had brought with them a troop of chess knights. The horse-like figurines neighed at the words, hinting that they could climb on top of them. As soon as they all had one word on their backs, they started riding. Moving fast in L-shape motion and jumping over the bolts, the knights galloped away from the woods, taking as many words as they could to a safe place.

But there were still many other words left there, and there came a point when they were overpowered by the rain of bolts. Everyone's strength was withering, that is until they became aware they were not alone in the line of defence. A formation of synonyms had come to stand for all the words Pox was destroying. *Loyalty* came to take the place of *devotion*. *Fate* replaced *destiny* and *longing* assumed the position of *desire*. *Stillness* aided *quietness*. *Work* rushed to help *labour*. When *beautiful* was killed, *gorgeous* came to the rescue. *Idea* stood in for *thought* and *talent* for *skill*. *Reason* covered both for *motive* and for *logic*.

Pox hated what he saw. Language was stronger than he'd imagined. It was protecting itself. He clenched his teeth and fury gushed from his goggled eyes. Sweat trickled down his face as he unleashed the most awful screech. He took all that rage and aimed it at the words that had no synonym.

Grandpa Davey fell to the ground when Pox shot down the name *Winifred*. Florence threw her shield on the ground and ran to help him up. The imp grinned and moved on to destroy the word *Inkwell*. For a second, nobody moved or uttered a word. The woods suddenly grew even darker.

Florence closed her eyes and dropped her head down. "No, no, no," she said. "This can't be happening." When she managed to open her eyes again, she saw that hope had faded.

"The battle's lost," Percival said.

"What's there to fight for now?" Lorelai sunk her head in her hands.

"Nothing, there's nothing left for us to do," Percival said. "It's over."

"Wait!" Ignatius said. "Listen…"

Everyone shushed.

"Is that who I think it is?" Imogen asked.

To stand in for *Inkwell*, for *Winifred* and for all the words that didn't have a synonym, the tribe of wombats from the Great Grumbling Grassland came striding. The pounding was loud and unswerving. They struck their drums with their paws making their tumbling beat travel through the ground and the air.

RUM PA PA PUMP!

POOM POOM POOM!

RUM PA PA PUMP!

RUM PA PA PUMP!

POOM POOM POOM!

The sound flooded the battlefield. Pox was suddenly thrown off balance. The drums were not only covering for the words without synonyms but were also scaring the wits out of

Pox. He dropped his crossbow and just stood still.

As the imp was about to recover, the Feather Farmers were quick to make their move. Each one had one feather in the palm of their hand. At the same time, they all blew upon them. The feathers made their way to Pox. Whirling around him, the feathers made Pox utterly dizzy in time, till he finally dropped to the ground.

At Florence's request, a hollow opened in the Wide Woeful Tree.

From its darkness, Zyler walked out. The wombats brought the drumming to a halt. The sorceress stood defiant, with her fearsome beauty, her intimidating dark eyes and her long red hair. She wore her warrior helmet and her black cape swished in the wind.

"She doesn't look as weak as *Lacuna Lares* described," Grandpa Davey whispered.

"She's been mustering strength every time the moon sparked off the spell," Florence said and took a step forward.

As history had once seen it, the Word-Keeper and the Word-Destroyer set eyes on each other once more. The night wind swept around the willows. It deadened all noises and stirred up the scent of bitter tree sap.

It was Florence who spoke first. "I will give you the choice, Zyler: choose the right path, stop what you are doing, or choose not to be at all."

Zyler sighed and with a mirthless smile she said, her eyes boring into her rival, "What name does the new Word-Keeper bear?"

The Word-Keeper answered without taking her eyes off Zyler either. "The name is Florence."

"Florence, are you ready to see your precious language be wiped out?"

"Never, we will get our…"

Zyler waited in delight, knowing that the word *victory* had already been shot down by Pox. "What's the matter? You cannot name it?" The sorceress said.

"I don't need to name it. I know it will be ours. There's nothing you can do that will stop us from stopping you. Your cruelness has only carried you this far. You won't go further with your hate."

"And you need so many to defeat me?" Zyler's voice was screechy. It contained the effects of Alodie's spell. It sounded like the voice of the oldest lady on Earth.

"We fight side by side. Unlike you, none of us is alone. We will always stand together."

Florence clasped her hands with Grandpa Davey on her right and Hephy on her left. They in turn held hands with Mr Caroling, Mr McGlue, Ignatius, Jakob, Imogen and Monsieur Pépite. The first circle was formed around Zyler and Pox.

A second circle of Inkwellers took shape around the first, then a third one around the second. A fourth circle was further forged by the Feather Farmers. The fifth circle was locked by the joining hands of Melvin and all the inventors of the Riveting River Valley. Around them, the wombats and their drums were blaring like thunder. The Pedantic Plum Trees interwove their branches to close the final circle, making it impossible for Pox or Zyler to get out of there.

When the last hand was held, Florence said, looking straight into Zyler's eyes, "Your imp has hurt so many words, but our language knows no bound. It can never be drained. If you think you can stop us, you are mistaken."

Florence's voice was joined by all others. Together they pronounced the most heroic words that were still left in the human language. And they were countless.

Life, Reason, Poetry, Grace
Moonlight, Man, Time, Embrace,
Mother, Father, Oath, Earth,
Son, Daughter, Bond, Worth,
Fearless, Candour, Journey, Story,
Warmth, Touch, Fairest, Glory,
Fellowship, Brotherhood, Virtue, Will,
Sunshine, Beauty, Limitless, Quill,
Dreamlike, Praise, Forgive, Rise,
Teacher, Insight, Self, Wise,
Answer, Justice, Dearest, Greatness,
Soul, Breath, Achievement, Purpose,
Birth, Thought, Value, Try,
Highest, Sacred, You and I.

The sound of words together with the wombats' drums pierced through the sorceress and surrounded her like a thick barrier. It was deadlier than any bullet ever shot and stronger than any barricade ever made before that day. The Word-Destroyer could not move. Her face went pale and started cracking; her skin looked scorched. Her eyes lost all intensity. Her hands were quivering and her red hair faded to a dull grey.

She tried to resist, clutching on to the last remnants of her evil spirit. A whirlwind of fog sheathed her. The power of the words was too strong. It wiped every ounce of her villainy out of existence and dried Zyler to her core until there was nothing else left except ashes that the wind took away.

Pox squirmed in the ground. He screeched in pain and wriggled his body from side to side, flailing wildly in despair. After one last mournful scream, he disappeared into a puff of greenish smoke.

෨

Ben appeared, lying on the ground when the smoke cleared. Florence's heart stood still for a second. She ran to him and kneeled by his side. She gently put him on the palm of her hand.

"Ben… Ben, are you all right?" Florence asked softly.

Ben wouldn't move. His little body was like a rag doll. His eyes were closed.

"Oh no, no!" Florence said. "Please, Ben, don't go. Don't leave us."

Grandpa Davey took both hands to his heart. Mr Caroling closed his eyes. So did Mr McGlue. A whimper slipped out of Monsieur Pépite's mouth, "*Le pauvre!*"

The wombats put down their drums and bowed their heads. The inventors from the Riveting River Valley stood in complete stillness.

Hephy was the one who stepped forward, walked to where Florence was and kneeled beside her. She placed her hand on Florence's shoulder and said the only thing she could say in that moment, "I'm so sorry, Florence."

Florence stroked Ben's forehead and rearranged his big pleated cap.

"Is this the end to our crusade?" Florence asked and relied on her silence to find the answer. "If today is the day I have to see you go, let it be known, Ben, that you were the bravest warrior, the finest bookmark, and the worthiest friend."

When Florence said this, she felt a slight jiggle in her palm. She looked down and not only did she feel it but she saw it. Ben's hands were wiggling.

"Ben?" she asked, trying not to get too attached to hope. "Ben, are you all right?" Her voice was a whisper, as if speaking aloud might cause the wiggling to stop.

Ben opened his eyes. "I'm so happy to see you again," he said with his courtly manner. Grandpa Davey cheered as if someone had made the loudest noise eating a handful of toasted almonds.

"Florence?" Ben said.

"Yes?"

"Has the spell been broken?"

"Yes, Ben, it has. Zyler's gone and so is Pox."

"Look everyone!" Hephy had stood up and was looking all around her.

"What is this?" Lorelai asked.

The sun was rising, and with it, green stems were growing everywhere. The trees had stopped crying. It was as if they'd awoken from a long and torturing nightmare. Their highest branches tinkled with bright light which then spiralled down their trunks. The ghostly mist had faded and the air was fresh. All quicksand and rotten deadfall disappeared and gave way to clearings of sweet-scented flowers.

"This...was us," Florence said.

"What do you mean?" Hephy asked her.

"Our fight. When I read Alodie's last message, I understood something: if good and evil are fighting to see one winner but the battle is fought with violence, evil will prevail and no heroes will be found, for no matter who wins, evil's own nature is being used to fight."

"If violence steers the way forward, the wrong-doers win the fight before starting," Ignatius said.

"This," Florence said, pointing to the woods, "is our gift for facing our enemy without violence."

"But then how did you defeat them?" Ben asked.

"The circles," Hephy said.

"Exactly," Florence said. "Union. That's what Alodie's message was all about, and that's what the robins and the nightingales sang. The circles we forged, we found a way to make dawn and dusk hold hands. All of us together, with our hands, our voices, our words, we made an unbreakable chain."

158

"I don't think the Wide Woeful Tree will be woeful again," Imogen said, walking towards all the poppies and peonies that now surrounded the tree.

"Then it should have a new name: Wide Winsome Tree," Percival said.

"I like that," Mr McGlue said.

"Come on, our town is waiting. It's time to go home," Grandpa Davey said.

The Feather Farmers, the Pedantic Plum Trees and the inventors went back west, to the Valley, the Pathway and the Fields. Everyone else turned back to head east to Inkwell.

They were almost out of the woods when Ben saw that a glade of dandelions had bloomed where only heartache and slime-coated rocks existed before.

"Are those…" he started to ask.

"Alodie's dandelions?" Florence finished for him. "What do you think?"

"I think they are."

"I think so too."

Hephy, who was walking ahead, turned around and waited for them.

"Florence, can you hear it?" she asked.

"I can."

"The trees aren't sad any more. They're singing."

"And whispering friendly words."

Of Garden Parties and Happy Words

A full moon bathed Inkwell in a silver light. There were frost swirls coating the windows of every cottage and puffs of warm smoke curling out of the chimneys. A gentle wind carried the scent of nearby pine needles.

A week had passed since Zyler and Pox were defeated. As the town got ready to celebrate, Florence was in her room sitting on the rocking chair, staring through the window. The moonlight made the snow on the crown of the trees glitter in the distance. While she basked in that view, she mused on all that had happened.

All the words Pox had destroyed had been born into existence once more when the imp was vanquished. One sentence at a time, the words found their place within the books. The good words that had camouflaged inside ugly words came out of hiding. *One* left *alone*, *here* walked out of *nowhere*, *eat* slipped out of *sweat*, *ace* emerged from *grimace* and *cat* sauntered out of *catastrophe*, stretched out and purred.

Florence got up from the rocking chair and as she dressed up for the party, she remembered what she'd told the town that morning in the main square when she climbed up the maple tree: "The words will find the way back to their place." She had kept her promise and *victory* was theirs.

She combed her hair and painted her fingernails with ruby-red nail polish because things in life always looked better with ruby-red nail polish. Before going downstairs to join the party, she stopped in the doorway of her room and took a long look at the bookshelves. The books were safe now, and so were the stories within them. A smile twinkled across Florence's eyes.

෨

In the kitchen, Ben was helping Grandpa Davey prepare that night's dinner because the party was going to be held in the cottage.

"Listen, Ben," Grandpa Davey said, looking at the little bookmark running around, all worried about getting everything right. "It's good to learn. And we learn by doing and trying, but may I give you a slice of advice?"

"Of course."

"Are you paying attention?"

"Uh-huh."

"Really paying attention?"

"Uh-huh."

"Will you always remember what I'm about to tell you?"

"Uh-huh."

"And never forget it?"

"Wouldn't that be the same as always remembering it?"

"It would. I just needed to double-check."

"Then, yes, I will never forget it."

And Grandpa Davey said, "Don't take life too seriously."

Ben stared at him. His eyes narrowed. He looked at Grandpa Davey as if trying to let him know he'd never fathomed that possibility, "Are you serious?"

"I'm always serious about not taking life too seriously."

Ben's eyes rolled up to a corner and stayed there as he measured the idea. "Do not take life too seriously... Hmm." He wasn't too convinced about that. Life was a serious matter.

That's what he'd always thought anyway. Was there another way to take life?

Ben scratched the back of his neck and repeated the phrase at a slow pace: "Do not take life too seriously... Hmm... Hmm." This time something about that advice tickled him. So he said it again, in a louder voice and at an even slower pace, almost at the speed of an elderly, grey-haired snail: "*Do...not... take...life...too...seriously.*"

Silence.

Maybe there was another way to take life after all. He pictured different scenarios where he'd approach life with this attitude.

"I like the prospects of this advice. I'll give it a try."

"By this I don't mean you can do as you please," Grandpa Davey said. "By this I mean that life is too good to waste your time being upset or uptight or uneasy. Life has to feel comfortable, like a tailored suit."

"Or a fluffy sweater," Ben said.

"Even better," Grandpa Davey said. "Today we are having a celebration feast, so whatever we do, we need to do it worry-free, OK? Remember, we do not give way to edginess and we never ever allow our mind to dwell on troubles."

&

All the town had dressed up. They were all groomed and ready to party. Ruffles and sequins, silk satin dresses and bow ties, peaked lapels and handkerchiefs neatly folded in suit pockets. Even the two sheep that were always roaming around Grandpa Davey's garden, who by that time had been officially baptized Zelda and Zelia, were wearing two little fancy velour hats tilted on top of their heads.

One by one they all arrived at Grandpa Davey's cottage. Although it was the middle of the winter, it had stopped snowing. The night was friendly and not too cold so the party was held in the garden lit by a round full moon.

Grandpa Davey had made a banana barbecue, a dish everyone was secretly hoping he'd make since he only prepared it for very special occasions.

Monsieur Pépite was so excited to have his recipe book again he prepared seventy-nine melt-in-your-mouth, finger-licking treats that included chocolate cakes, chocolate muffins, chocolate mousse, chocolate truffles, chocolate cupcakes, chocolate scones, chocolate pie and chocolate tart, which no one really knew what the difference was, and chocolate-covered peppermint patties.

They all sat down at a long table. Ben crammed large pieces of banana barbecue into his mouth and let himself be carried away with bliss. Trevor and Jakob wolfed down chocolate cupcakes as if there was no tomorrow. The two robins and the two nightingales stopped by and pecked at the scones.

Florence made her special velvety vanilla cake. All the guests ate a piece and laughed madly all the way through the party. Lorelai and Ignatius couldn't resist the temptation and ate three pieces. They went on to guffaw for two days straight.

Dinner was not divided, as it usually is, in sections such us appetizers, main course and dessert. The rule of the night was "Be it sweet or salty, eat whatever you crave in the order you wish." Some ate *sweet, savoury, sweet.* A few were more classic and started with *savoury* and then moved on to *sweet,* and a handful chose a very repetitive sequence of *sweet, sweet, sweet* all the way to the end, the end being a bellyache and a sugar rush.

"The library's in order again!" Lorelai shouted at one point during the evening.

"Talk about order! I've found the rhyme my poems had lost!" Percival said.

"To Inkwell and its Word-Keeper!" Mr McGlue said as he raised his glass.

"To Inkwell and its Word-Keeper!" everyone cheered.

Later, the wombats played the drums. Everyone jumped, stamped the ground and swung their arms around. Hephy and Florence danced together while eating cupcakes. Ben went around the dance floor attempting to dance and not get squashed in the process. Trevor and Jakob continued munching. After devouring the last chocolate scones, they moved on to the chocolate-covered peppermint patties which they spread with abundant chocolate mousse.

Little by little, as the music died down, as the food disappeared and as the feet got too swollen, the party reached its end. One by one, the same way they had arrived, the guests left. But not empty handed. Trevor took home a bowl of chocolate mousse. Mr McGlue made sure to take some of the banana barbecue for next day's breakfast and Grandpa Davey gave the wombats the remaining truffles for their journey back to the grasslands. Florence and Hephy hugged goodbye and then Florence promised to stop by Scriptoria Hill before going back to the city.

When all the guests had gone home, a soothing quietness was left in the cottage. With the help of Florence and Ben, Grandpa Davey set the cottage in order. But they took their time. It was as if a part of them didn't wish to erase all evidence of such a great party.

When all was tidy again, they went upstairs, said goodnight to one another and went to bed. Ben slept inside *The Adventures of Tom Sawyer* once again. Now that the words were back, Ben would be able to dream worry-free in the book.

Grandpa Davey put his pyjamas and his comfy sleep cap on and closed his eyes, and Florence closed hers under Grandma Winifred's hand-knitted quilt.

෨

At dawn Florence was the first one to wake up. She opened *The Adventures of Tom Sawyer* where Ben was sleeping. She didn't want to wake him up, so she carefully placed him on the desk. Ben tossed and turned and then went on snoring.

Without making too much noise, she got dressed, grabbed her book, wrapped herself with the hand-knitted quilt and went outside. She sat on a bench in the garden. As the first rays of the sun hit her face, Florence closed her eyes and felt its warmth. Zelda and Zelia came to say hello and then kept on strolling along Grandpa Davey's yard, eating grass and looking solemnly amused.

She opened *The Adventures of Tom Sawyer* and gazed at the words. She didn't start reading at once. She wanted to take a good, long look at each one of the words on the page.

"It's good to have you back," she said to them.

As much as she'd enjoyed reading so many books in the past, that morning was the one she enjoyed the most. She kept on reading until the sun was halfway up the sky, until Grandpa Davey and Ben were awake and making breakfast.

When Ben called her because Grandpa Davey had just taken the Colossal Croissants out of the oven, Florence was holding the closing page. The kettle in the kitchen was whistling and that meant three cups of tea would soon be ready to be poured.

After reading *present*, the last word of *The Adventures of Tom Sawyer*, she closed the book and was certain of three things: 1) She would still publicly declare her undying love for salted hazelnuts in brown paper bags, warm milk with tons of honey and lumpy mashed potatoes with nutmeg. 2) The itchy feeling that loomed on windy nights telling her that something was missing in her life was forever gone. And 3) As the Word–Keeper, she would make sure no word was bashed, belittled or forsaken under her watch.

Back in the City

When Florence got back home she told her parents all that had happened. They gave her such a long questioning look that Florence thought it would never end. Fact-loving mathematicians they were, it was hard for them to swallow the news.

Her mother's questioning look faded when she remembered the old saying: "*Once the train crosses the Arcane Bridge, you have to be ready for the uncanny, the untold and the unimaginable.*" Then she also remembered she'd once lived in Inkwell. She thought of the bookshop and the main square with the maple tree and the water well. It suddenly dawned on her that what had happened with her daughter was actually the most logical thing in the world.

For Mr Percy Ibbot it took a little more time.

"An evil sorceress? A wicked imp? A bookmark that comes to life?" he asked himself aloud as he scratched his head. "Spells? A book with blank pages that reveals stories only to the right reader? Words being butchered by bolts?" He scratched his head again. "My daughter? A genie? A Word-Keeper?"

When he uttered those three last sentences, there were no more questions: there was a memory. He remembered the first word Florence uttered: *hyperbole.* He'd always believed Florence had peculiar qualities that made her what they in the maths world liked to call *out of the ordinary*. And then it hit him: out of the ordinary did not equal impossible. Out of the ordinary equalled extraordinary. The questions turned into facts: "My daughter! A genie! A Word-Keeper!" He even left numbers aside for a while and dived head first into the world of literature (only for a while, he eventually went back to the world of maths, which after all is also a beautiful language).

∞

Back at school, Florence didn't tell anyone what had happened. It was easier for her to do her job if no one knew who she really was.

First task ahead: Gideon Green. Time to put her power to good use.

It happened during Miss Malloy's geometry class. The blackboard was covered with problems. Questions like *How many different triangles can you find in a circle that has eight points spaced evenly on the circumference?* kept everyone terribly busy, ruler and pencil in hand. Florence turned around from her desk and faced Gideon.

"Hey," she said.

"What?" he snapped back.

"I want to tell you something."

"Well, I don't want you to tell me anything, geek. Scram!"

"Too bad, because today you will listen to what I have to say," Florence said. She leaned in closer to him and whispered something near his ear. Gideon froze for three seconds and then went back to normal. Florence turned back and continued working on her geometry problems.

From that moment on, every time Gideon wanted to bother someone with a mean comment he would instead say things like "Well done!" or "Genius!" or "Right on!" or "Kudos to you for that awesome answer!" At first he got raging

168

mad for saying exactly the opposite to what he'd intended to say. After the tenth time it happened, he gave up. After the twentieth time, it began to grow on him. He found it quite agreeable to say nice things to his classmates. By the thirtieth time, he had become really good at it and Florence's spell was not even necessary any more.

Second task ahead: the Quarrelsome Queens.

Needless to say, Tabitha, Tallulah and Luella hadn't changed their ways one bit. They were still conceited, addicted to gossiping and very much bossing everyone around.

In the playground there was a chestnut tree. The Quarrelsome Queens had decided long ago that that was their spot and no one could come near it unless an invitation was extended. Florence disregarded that rule and walked right under the chestnut tree where the three of them were gossiping as usual.

"What do you think you are doing?" Tabitha said.

"There's something you need to know," Florence said.

"You haven't been invited here! Leave before–" Luella said.

"Before what?" Florence asked.

"This is *our* tree!" Tabitha shouted.

"It won't be for long." Florence came closer to the Quarrelsome Queens and whispered:

> *May your voice become a twin*
> *Of the soul you bear within.*
> *May your tongue follow your heart*
> *While your call just falls apart.*
> *Your lips will cry an ending squall*
> *And you'll be shunned by one and all.*
> *When Northern Winds at last arrive*
> *Your masks will fall, so will your pride.*

The Quarrelsome Queens froze for three seconds. When they came around from that swift daze, Florence wasn't there any more. A cold wind blew strong. The flag on top of the mast in the playground was pointing south. The branches of the chestnut tree rattled madly and more than a few leaves left the tree and glided down to the ground.

The bell rang and all the students hurried back to class. The day went on, and as it did, the Quarrelsome Queens noticed there was something wrong with their voices. No matter what they said, people looked at them in horror and ran away. The more they spoke, the lonelier they became.

"What's wrong with us?" Tabitha said.

"Just hear us!" Luella said.

"What are we going to do?" Tallulah asked.

"Well," Florence told them, "looks like your voices now match your personality."

From then on, everyone heard them as they truly were. Their commands lost all power and Tabitha, Tallulah and Luella were left without victims. Their reign had finally come to an end.

EPILOGUE

(or within the part of the book where the story continues just a little bit longer)

Ben stayed in Inkwell. He lived there during the year when Florence was in the city and awaited every December when she came back.

During the time she was away, he helped Grandpa Davey in the bookshop. He was very polite with the customers and had a fine technique for wrapping up the books that were meant to be presents. If he had time in between customers, he browsed the Theatre section, chose a scene from a play and performed it aloud, taking on all the roles.

On Saturdays, he helped Monsieur Pépite in his chocolate shop. This, Ben liked a lot. The perks of working in a chocolate shop were many and they all involved eating. He baked for a while and then ate a spoonful of chocolate mousse. He took a batch of brownies out of the oven and helped himself to one or two. And before heading back home to Grandpa Davey's cottage, he always stuffed his pockets with chocolate truffles.

He didn't forget about his dreams. Grandpa Davey gave him a parcel of the garden where Ben cleverly laid out his O farm with ostriches, otters, owls and orangutans and a pond with octopuses, orcas and oysters. It became world-renowned and animals travelled all the way to Inkwell just to see if there would be a place for them there. Grandpa Davey had to give Ben a bigger patch of the garden because the O farm had also become the home of an oryx, an ocelot, two oxen and a flock of osprey.

Ben got to be the skipper of a fishing boat, stand behind the tiller and have an adventure at sea. Well, not exactly at sea, but at a quite large freshwater lake in the Wood of Whispering Weeping Willows. He sailed in a little boat he built with his own hands. It had poplin sails and a tin-plate mast. He painted the hull red and blue. Oddly rigged and rusty, it did look like a quintessential fishing boat.

Ben also went to the Great Grumbling Grassland every Thursday to meet with Bert, a bumblebee known as the best ukelele player in the region. He had been introduced to Ben by the bongo-playing wombats.

"Any song is a happy song when played with a ukelele," Bert told Ben during the first lesson. "If you are sad, the ukelele will make you happy, and if you are happy, happier and happier you'll get. It's like eating mangos on top of a palm tree or dipping sponge ladyfingers in your strawberry milkshake."

The only thing left in his dreams-to-come-true list was becoming a champion dominoes player, but the vacant slots left by the dreams that had already come true were quickly filled with new ones: become a cricket umpire, learn to run like an Olympic athlete and attempt to be a reporter for a morning gazette.

ဆ

After so many years, Grandpa Davey got a letter from Mr Quill. In it, he wrote all about that invitation to journey beyond the Mountains of the East.

Hazel Lands was the name of the town he had travelled to and where he, in fact, still lived. The letter was packed with the wildest stories that happened in this faraway place. But…that's for another story entirely.

ဆ

Jakob found the idea he had lost many years ago when Grandpa

Davey met him in the Great Grumbling Grassland. Since then, he'd written other stories, but not a day went by when he thought about that story that had got away.

One evening, as he was making his way to one of Ben's ukelele concerts, a seed from one of the dandelions that had bloomed in the Wood of Whispering Weeping Willows landed on his head...

ZOOMMM!

There it was.

This time Jakob didn't let go of it. He grabbed it, put it in his pocket and ran home to start writing. He didn't leave his house for weeks. In fact, he barely rose from his desk. Quill in hand, eyes on the paper, ink pot nearby, he wrote without rest as his story unfolded. It would turn out to be one of the greatest novels ever written.

&

Grandpa Davey finally discovered his favourite word.

He was in his garden trying a new trick on his penny-farthing bike. When he finally nailed it to perfection, he wanted to yell this one-syllable word out loud. He jumped off the bike and ran into the kitchen.

"I've finally found it!" he said to Ben.

"Are you talking about...?"

"Yes! My word!"

"Well, what are you waiting for? Tell me!"

Grandpa Davey grabbed his pen and a piece of paper and he traced the first letter: B... Without lifting the tip of the pen, the rest of the letters trickled down onto the paper.

"*Brill*!" Ben read.

"First and foremost, *brill* rhymes with *quill*," Grandpa Davey said. "And not only was that the name of my teacher, but it's also the word assigned to all the pens made of tail feathers with which great stories were written."

"Don't know if you know, but *brill* is also a funny-looking flatfish," Ben added.

"And on top of all that, the word has a b and two ls in it, it's short for *brilliant* and it's usually used with an exclamation mark at the end. A great word to finish a thought, a sentence or a story."

℘

Just like Alodie, Florence mastered the art of wordsmithing. She could craft words when and if a situation required it. Once a word was created, it leaked down into the world, people picked up on it and began using it.

She crafted words like *velarins* for those dreams that one would like to dream again and *tuzzies* for the pigs that managed to stay spotless in the pigpen. She created the word *lameelos* to define sad memories that decided to creep in when one was having fun and *alaphee* to talk about a morning that smelled like night-time. *Paploons* were the unavoidable women with severely exaggerated puffed-out hairdos, *finamures* were the birds that had no sense of decency and sang when one was trying to take a nap, and *queeblos* were the drawers in a cupboard that were always packed with useless stuff.

She discovered that there was a need for a word to define the songs that one could listen to over and over again and never get tired of them, so she named them *loozies*, and *marfins* were the corn kernels that would refuse to puff up and become popcorn no matter how long one left them on the stove, remaining unpopped popcorn forever. She fashioned the word *wogis* to define the days when no matter what one did, one did not look pretty and *zoobats* for the people with really bushy eyebrows.

As for *Lacuna Lares*, it remained in Florence's care since she now knew how to read it. The book found safekeeping in her hands, cautiously revealing answers solely to her.

On the night she got back from Inkwell, Florence got in her bed, opened *Lacuna Lares* and found a third message from Alodie:

> You are the Word-Keeper now. Let everyone know that as a man speaks, so he lives. Make the right choices regarding language and take action against those who do wrong by the words. Remind human beings that when it comes to words, they can be their strongest ally or their greatest threat, and they should always choose to be the first.

And so it was that from then on, Florence Ibbot devoted her time to building an understanding of the world using words. Her presence was felt in every domain and province. It reached the most hidden and remote nooks of the globe, reminding everyone that much in the universe is held together with words.

Thank you

Helen Hart, Anna Loo, and the entire team at SilverWood Books – for supporting me every step of the way;

Kate Haigh – for your impeccable proofreading;

Eleanor Hardiman – for your exquisite illustrations;

Elise Valmorbida – for guiding me through the beginnings of this book with your wisdom and expertise;

Adam Baron, James Miller, and Norma Clarke – for your brilliant insights, knowledge and talent;

My fellow writers at Kingston University – for your feedback and inspiration;

Bonny, JJ and Billy – for 39 years of love and happy moments;

Ale Cavallo – for reading so many versions of this story and for being so awesome;

Clau Mosovich, Agus La Ruffa and Ivi Hechem, my most excellent friends – for your invaluable advice;

And Alistair Whitlock – for reminding me to be strong and live a great life.

Lightning Source UK Ltd.
Milton Keynes UK
UKHW012225030519
342082UK00001B/40/P